CW01395430

Blair J Collins was born and bred in Essex, close to the Thames River. This is his first work of prose fiction. He spent the majority of his working life in the fire service, retiring recently to concentrate on his writing.

Blair and his partner divide their time between the UK and Germany.

To Klaudia, with love.

Blair J Collins

A COASTAL SHELF

AUSTIN MACAULEY PUBLISHERS®

LONDON * CAMBRIDGE * NEW YORK * SHARJAH

Copyright © Blair J Collins 2024

The right of Blair J Collins to be identified as author of this work has been asserted by the author in accordance with sections 77 and 78 of the Copyright, Designs and Patents Act 1988.

All rights reserved. No part of this publication may be reproduced, stored in a retrieval system, or transmitted in any form or by any means, electronic, mechanical, photocopying, recording, or otherwise, without the prior permission of the publishers.

Any person who commits any unauthorised act in relation to this publication may be liable to criminal prosecution and civil claims for damages.

This is a work of fiction. Names, characters, businesses, places, events, locales, and incidents are either the products of the author's imagination or used in a fictitious manner. Any resemblance to actual persons, living or dead, or actual events is purely coincidental.

A CIP catalogue record for this title is available from the British Library.

ISBN 9781035823437 (Paperback)
ISBN 9781035823444 (ePub e-book)

www.austinmacauley.com

First Published 2024
Austin Macauley Publishers Ltd®
1 Canada Square
Canary Wharf
London
E14 5AA

I would like to thank the following people:

Ben Kelly, my first reader. For persevering with the first rough draft on his phone before providing a constructive and balanced critique.

To my daughter, Sarah, for her unwavering help and belief in my work that far exceeded my own.

To my other children, Joanne and Neil.

Finally and most importantly, Klaudia Seitz. For all the love.

Copyright Acknowledgements

The Complete Poems by Philip Larkin, Faber & Faber Ltd, reproduced by permission of the Publisher.

Excerpts from "Aubade," "An Arundel Tomb," "This Be The Verse," and "The Trees" from THE COMPLETE POEMS OF PHILIP LARKIN by Philip Larkin, edited by Archie Burnett. Copyright © 2012 by The Estate of Philip Larkin. Reprinted by permission of Farrar, Straus and Giroux. All Rights Reserved.

Prologue

There had been a heat wave. The local authorities had to impose a hosepipe ban on a hot and vexed community. The county's lakes needed to be oxygenated with fresh water to prevent the fish dying and around the countryside, plumes of dusty grey smoke rose in the cloudless skies as grass and heath succumbed to the carelessness of folk and the inveterate arsonist.

The summer roads of Essex had been burnished from the countless tyres during this particular arid month. On this day, a late afternoon at the end of June, Ursula and Eve were travelling back home from their shopping expedition to Southend on Sea.

The two close friends had lunch in Tomassi's, then picked up the last few things they needed for their weekend away at a book festival in the West Country. Driving home, they spoke animatedly about the camp site where they would sleep in the VW, cook on the Primus stove and dance around a campfire.

"Oh, to be young again," said Ursula.

"Young, free and single," came the reply. "Hippies! Carefree hippies," said Eve as she wound down the window, feeling the wind in her hair.

It started to rain. The carriageway exuded a film of oil undermining the trust placed in it by the motorists. The lorry driver travelling in the opposite direction to Ursula and Eve cursed as his windscreen steamed up. The day had been long for this hard-working man and he still had one more delivery of rolled steel joists to a site in Chalkwell.

Lighting a cigarette, he noticed the VW camper van ever so close to the central white line. Perhaps, he knew later, he would never forget, he should not have made a quick downward pull on the steering wheel that resulted in the loss of traction on the treacherous surface and his subsequent overreaction that sent the articulated lorry sliding across the road.

His cab hit Ursula's VW van a glancing blow that would kill Ursula outright. The trailer jack-knifed behind him and trapped Eve with sickening ease in her front seat for an excruciating hour while attempts were made to free her until she too succumbed to her injuries.

The rain, channelled by the kerbstones, gurgled as it entered the drains. The road steamed, drying quickly and the afternoon air had a purity so desired by the photographer. Metal contracted and flexed noisily, unsure of its new form. A gardener would turn to her husband and smile, pleased the lawn had had a soaking. Within the hour, it was as if it had not rained at all.

Chapter 1

The air was chill. Any heat accumulation from the spring day had long escaped under the cloudless night sky. They were putting out another car fire. The fourth that night; six was not unusual. They were stolen in the city just for the ride home then torched.

Obviously cheaper than a cab and a low enough level of crime that meant any follow up that resulted in a prosecution was virtually non-existent. This vehicle left casually half on the pavement was a burnt-out shell when Eddie Hart and his crew of three arrived on the water tender from Langden fire station.

The water tender of which Eddie was in charge of was the station workhorse dealing with all the run of the mill calls, leaving the specialist appliances in the station for the bigger or more complex jobs.

They parked up wind from the toxic filth emanating from the vehicle and proceeded with one hose reel to extinguish what was left of the tyres and wiring loom.

"Crowbar the boot, Billy," said Eddie. "You never know." Eddie knew though how unprofessional it would be if later something untoward like a body was found inside, it had been known.

The police rocked up as requested. Suspicion of a crime, in this case arson was enough to ask for them. He watched them out of their car. This was the first time he had seen this pair tonight. *Coppers,* he thought, *we're not a lot different to fire-fighters, some were good, and some were shit. These two came in the latter category.*

"Evening."

"Alright."

They walked up to the car for a cursory glance and noted the legible number plate. Eddie watched as Jim who was holding the hose reel, clocked them coming and gradually manoeuvred himself to the opposite side of the vehicle from them. His jet of water might be hitting the burn out but the spray was going their way.

"Have you the RO?" Eddie asked the more senior copper and the surliest.

"Nah, can't give you that, I'm afraid."

"Yer other mates always give me the registered owner."

"Well, they shouldn't and we know what ya fuckin mate was trying to do with his hose."

"I know what he is trying to fuckin do as well he is trying to put out a fuckin fire."

Eddie wasn't in the mood for bridge building tonight. It had been one job after another. They had hardly been in the station since they started six hours ago and there was another nine in front of them. Eddie turned his back on the coppers as they drove off and watched as his crew went about their work.

Watching was important. To watch out for one another. No matter how mundane a task. Certain car components had the habit of exploding, petrol dripping from a fractured line underneath the vehicle could ignite and carried on the water, produce a river of flame at unsuspecting heels.

Jim was working the hose reel jet into the car's hidden nooks and crannies. It may be a given that the fire service put fires out but it was essential they stayed out. A re-ignition was unprofessional and a chargeable offence. Jim worked the hose reel methodically back and forth, alternating from jet to spray.

Eddie watched. *No kids tonight,* he thought, as late as it was you could normally expect one or two teenagers on bikes loitering in the shadows. Equally, no neighbour leaning against a front door, watching in idle fascination, enjoying the last fag before bed.

He surveyed the estate, all windows were shut. The occupants of the oddly shaped, award winning flats had smelt the acrid tang of smoke in the cool night air and knew what to do.

Billy Butler, after some levering, thumping and grunting had popped the boot. He stared into the emptiness. He knew the chances of finding something exciting therein was unlikely but Eddie was right, you never knew. What he did know as he stared down into the metal casing now devoid of its original fittings was how people today by and large drove without a jack and spare.

Harry completed the crew. He was the driver and ergo, the pump operator. He stood to the rear of the appliance, keeping an eye on the tank indicator. A clear tube attached to the back of the fire engine containing water and a ping pong ball. The height of the ball in the tube mirrored the level of water in the on-board tank. The ball was near the bottom of the tube when Harry Samuels shouted.

"Nearly empty."

Eddie walked over to Jim.

"We're nearly empty Jim, need more?"

"No, I'm done here."

"Ok," said Eddie, "let's find a hydrant fill up and fuck off."

When Eddie finished the last fire report, it was past nine. He filed his paperwork and was putting a few things in his locker when the man in charge of Red Watch, Arthur Church, stuck his head around the door to Eddie's room.

"The back is playing me up, Eddie," he said. "I'll have to see how it goes over the next few days but if I'm not in next tour, you will have to act up and we have the recruit starting. OK?"

"No problem guv, I hope you feel better soon." They both smiled. They had been a comfortable and easy-going team for some years now. Arthur was a shade taller than Eddie despite a slight stoop. His grey hair and poor posture aged him unkindly. He was only one year older than Eddie but had seen more service, transferring out of London ten years earlier.

"It was the travelling," he told Eddie. "Couldn't afford a house up there and London weighting made little difference to my income, as much as I loved it, I was getting fed up schlepping up town from Billericay then the transfer to Paddington was the straw that broke the proverbial."

"Their loss, Arthur."

"Yea, not sure our top floor feel the same."

Eddie had long admired Arthur's unswerving support for the men under his command and he never balked at taking the bosses to task when necessary. Eddie didn't always agree with his methods but it would be a bit creepy if he found no fault. Arthur Church turned gingerly, waving a goodbye as he went. Eddie took a look around his room, making sure he had everything before he too left the building.

The rest of Red Watch were already off home or to second jobs. The Blue were checking the lorries as Eddie crossed the yard to his car. Monday morning, sunny, warm, was the start of the week for the majority in this town. Now, the shops in the centre were starting to open.

People would be queuing outside the post office for pensions and stamps and throughout the estates, languid mothers walking back from the school drop off were pushing prams and in no hurry to return home to housework, TV and baby talk.

This was a populace of honest working class, solid Labour and aspiring Tories, of rogues and rebels of family dynasties, proud of their place and the London they left. This was a community of hardship and heartbreak of black eyes and bruises of laughter and a deep sense of belonging.

The people of Langden with the myriad things they had to do with the day in front of them would be starting this sunny Monday morning without a second thought to the state provided emergency services all a simple phone call away. Why should they give a second thought to say, the fire station?

The majority of people go through their entire life without having a fire. Who worries about road traffic collisions every time they turn over the engine or the likelihood of their property flooding? Who worries about a crisis that may never happen when there were mortgages to pay and children to clothe and the threat of factory closures?

The people of Langden had more important things to worry about. And yet across this urban landscape, someone would step outside their front door today and with a sharp intake of breath, knowing as it shuts behind them that the baby was inside.

Someone would leave a pot on the stove before going upstairs to another chore and forget about it until they smell burning. Another would pull out in front of the lorry believing the lorry was giving way. Some people, maybe today, would be making that call.

Eddie's tour had finished, no one had died or suffered injury. The Red had put out fires while the locals watched TV or slept. They had gone about their work unnoticed by the people they served. On this fine spring morning, he was at the opposite end of the social spectrum, for him it was the end of his working week and four days lay ahead in which to do whatever he wanted.

For the next four days, he would go about his business, pay some bills, do the chores, he would change from protector to protected, he would join them, become a member of the public. He also knew what he had to do first so he jumped in the Ford and set off to his father's.

Chapter 2

Eddie Hart's parents had left London with the offer of council accommodation in what until then was a small and charming village in Essex on the Thames corridor, Stanford le Hope. It was where Eddie on the newly built housing estate next to the village grew up, playing football in the road, fighting kids from the surrounding streets and being bored.

Bored was okay though, just as long as you were outside and bored. Stuck indoors on rainy days where the TV rarely worked and his parents at work was akin to detention.

Ray Hart, had worked in the Royal Mint in London, travelling up by train before it moved to Wales. Ray could have taken his family to Wales also. With the promise of continued work, his current position and salary guaranteed and housing thrown in, it was, his mother thought, an exciting proposition but the ever-unexceptional unexciting choice made by Ray was to stay put, comforted by the accent of East London close by and now permeating through the Essex countryside.

Ray got a job in the local shoe factory. He worked shifts and when Eddie was old enough, his mother got a job with a local solicitor who admired her command of the English language. When production of shoes moved further afield than the minting of coin, Ray ended up collecting coin at the Dartford tunnel tolls that linked Essex and Kent below the Thames and that's where he remained until retirement.

Eddie opened the back door and called out to his father.

"In here," came the reply from the living room. Eddie walked through the small kitchen into the living room that traversed the house from front to back. No room for best in these ex council rents. Ray sat in his chair, the same one he always sat in. He was reading the Daily Mail.

"How was your weekend, Dad?" He said, slumping down on the settee.

"Same ol, same ol," said his father, not looking up from the society pages. Eddie gave the slightest of nods, looking around the room. The coal fire of his youth was now faux electric. The chimney breast was still artexed in broken leather while the remainder of wall was covered in a garish green patterned wallpaper that Eddie always thought was just shy of perpendicular.

He remembered his mum putting it up. On the front window sill was a vase containing a bunch of yellow daffs his mother had bought all those years ago. Her left arm crossed her midriff and held her right elbow, she drew on her cigarette, blew the smoke towards the ceiling and looking at Eddie said, "They'll do."

She laughed and messed his hair. Looking out of the front window, Eddie noticed that the brick wall enclosing the substation opposite the house had been graffitied with the words 'FUCK IT'.

"That's nice," said Eddie.

"What?"

"The wall."

Ray just shrugged and carried on reading.

Eddie felt a pressure in his temple as he watched his dad read, he clenched his teeth. He wanted to smash the paper from his father's grasp. He wanted to shout, it wasn't his fault. He looked away. His gaze continued round to the cocktail bar.

The upper shelf, glass fronted to display the alcohol never to be drunk. Small china barrels labelled Whisky, Brandy and Rum and a glass flamingo containing God knows what. *How many years,* he thought. The TV next to the hearth and staring straight at his father was the most modern item in the room, it was Ray's constant companion now, only turned off for this interlude with the paper. A cloth holster hung over the arm of his chair, containing the remote. He recalled when that was his exclusive job.

"Turn it over, son."

"Tea?"

"Yea, gaw on," said Ray.

While Eddie waited for the kettle to boil, he looked out over the back garden now surrounded by a six-foot fence. When they first moved here, the gardens were separated by waist high rustic fences. On summer evenings, the neighbours on either side and at the bottom would gather to have a chat and a laugh. Trays of tea were brought out. Eddie was good at making tea. What caught his eye first though was a neat pile of red and white concrete slabs.

"The slabs, Dad."

"Yea, came Friday. The patio, remember."

He remembered the patio Mum always wanted.

"Thought you might give me a hand."

"Bit busy this week," Eddie said without thinking.

"No rush," said Ray.

Eddie left an hour later after popping over to the shops for his dad and telling him he'd sort out some days for the patio. He would ask Jim to give him a hand. Ray would object, thinking about the cost but he could get around that. He thought about the gym but then realised he was dog tired from a busy night. His flat beckoned and the silence he hated as a kid now seemed as companionable to him as the TV to his father.

Chapter 3

Alone in his office sat station commander Clarence Siddall. He had summoned the boss of the Blue and waited in dull apathy for the coming conversation. Clarence Siddall was a career first officer. This station, as far as Clarence Siddall was concerned, was a stepping stone for him to senior management at divisional then county level.

He would sit in this office, plotting his next career move. He constantly checked the vacant positions. Fire prevention, too esoteric, could easily get side-lined, he thought, and forgotten. Now communications, that was worth considering. What better way to promote one's self than in-charge of the Comms dept. He looked up from the screen.

"Morning, Station Officer."

"Morning, Guvnor," Len replied.

Lenny Duff had taken twenty years to make Station Officer and was proud to have achieved what to him was the pinnacle of his career with still enough years left to enjoy the position. He was Mr Fire Brigade and had the respect of the men on his watch. The Blue Watch.

"Everything OK, Len?"

"Er yea, guv. What like, me, or—"

"No Len, not you, the station. When you took over from the Red, everything alright?"

"Yea."

"Machines clean?"

"Yea."

"Paperwork done?"

"Yup."

"So everything's alright?"

Len was never one for games or gamesmanship but could tell his positive responses were having a negative effect on the station commander.

"The petty cash is two p out," he said and regretted it immediately so nullified his comment with, "But I'd be surprised if it weren't."

"Surprised?" asked Clarence Siddall.

"Com' on guv, the petty cash is always two p out. But if I catch the embezzler, you will be the first to know."

Len's attempt at levity fell like a line bag from the third floor of the tower. He could almost hear the thud of the canvas bag full of rope hitting the concrete. Clarence Siddall looked past Len out of the window. Church Road was bumper to bumper. The pavement empty.

"Anything else, guv?" asked Len, breaking the silence.

"Er no, no Len," said Clarence Siddall, only half listening.

"In that case guv, I was wondering about my leave this year and—"

"Not now, Len. I'm very busy. Put it in an email and that will be all."

Alone again in his office, the dissatisfaction he felt about life and career weighed heavily. What appeared effortless for his peer group as they rose through the ranks was hard work and rejection for him. He felt as if he was promoted as the last resort.

He tried hard with senior management but felt more used than abetted. He had the work ethic instilled in him by his father but that alone did not reap the rewards he craved. A pivotal moment was required. To be spoken of as the man that was responsible for putting out the biggest conflagration Essex had known or the officer that brought the toughest personnel problems under control. He continued looking at the vacancies and his route to the top but today his mind wouldn't settle to the task. He was elsewhere.

Clarence Siddall was taught by nuns until the age of eleven. He achieved average results academically as well as sportingly and there lay his problem, an average child. An unexceptional child who went unnoticed. So he was left alone which suited him. He knew school years had to be endured before he like his father could make his way in the world.

His mother doted on him and favoured him over his clever sibling. Aubrey Siddall had a Victorian attitude to life. He loved his son and daughter and what better way to show it than the accumulation of wealth and status to be endowed onto the next generation upon his demise. Clarence loved spending time with him, content in his shadow.

Together, they went to his father's factory. The deference his staff showed was polite and absolute. If he were lucky, he might be taken to the local lodge.

There he would sit quietly with a lemonade and watch as men shook hands, smoked cigars and planned their joint accumulation of wealth.

To his father's dismay, Clarence failed his eleven plus and as the door to the local Grammar closed, the gates of St Just Private School opened. His father had power and Clarence was given privilege but amongst the rest of the privileged, it counted for nought. What he never considered as he walked through the gates at the start of his first term was how his time there would wither his soul.

How the society of his fellow pupils would leech goodness from his marrow with every flick of a wet towel. How Siddall became sod all and ultimately fuck-all when the well-endowed bullies noticed how he showered with one hand cupped over his genitals.

Humiliation on the rugby field compounded in the showers as his arms were pinned to the tiled floor and cold water was played over his private shame to see if it could be made to disappear completely. The humiliation absolute when walking home past a group of his class and girls from the nearby convent school looked his way, whispered and laughed. A boy shouted, "See ya fuck all," as the laughter rose to a cacophony of adolescent ridicule.

He snapped himself out of his reverie and back to his current situation and how to garner enough credibility with senior management to necessitate his promotion. The Red were held in low esteem by the top floor. Considered unruly and disrespectful. *Who knows,* thought Clarence Siddall, *who knows.*

Chapter 4

The ringing phone woke Eddie with the same immediacy as a fire call. He sat bolt upright before realising the room's darkness meant he was at home and not at the station.

"Hi Eddie, did I wake you?"

"Hi Jane, no it's okay, just dozing. Busy night."

"Well, that's why they pay you the big bucks," she said.

"Yep, you got it," he said, the tone in his voice ladened with irony. "What do you want?"

"Oh Jane, nice to hear from you and how are you, how's work?" Jane could always match his irony and take it up a notch.

"Sorry Jane, you did wake me from a coma. Give me five and I'll call you back."

He showered quickly, squeegeed the cubicle dry before towelling himself, then in the kitchen he carefully filled the Bialetti Moka pot and placed it on the hob. While it percolated, he opened the cupboard and removed a white bone china mug. From the fridge he took milk, poured some into a milk saucepan and when it was warm, frothed it. He folded the foamy milk into the mug and added the coffee.

He picked up the phone, wondering what Jane wanted. She didn't phone so much these days so perhaps she needed a hand with something. He had known Jane Fleming since school. Eddie was in the third year at Branksome secondary modern when he heard of the arrival of a new girl. Same year but not the same class so he had to wait for a break to catch a curious glimpse in the school playground.

It was a mixed school but by and large, the sexes kept themselves separate apart from a few loved-up loners. He stood in a circle of mates while they looked down, admiring John's new shoes. Eddie's jealousy got the better of him when he said he didn't like them.

"Well, they're better than yours," said Alan, which made the whole gang laugh. They knew his dad worked in the shoe factory and brought shoes home for him that spoke more of his father's taste than the latest styles. Eddie wanted to walk away but knew he had to front it out and tried to laugh along.

It was then he noticed the group of girls. The girls that had the latest hair style, short dresses and beneath the tight white blouse wore bra's that, they or padding, modestly filled and which added to the allure that he and his mates were alive to.

Jane stood in the middle of this group, already accepted by them. It was so different for boys, acceptance had to be earned even fought for. She had got the uniform spot on though her blonde hair was longer, a high pony tail that had the length to lay over one shoulder. Her slight frame had the beginnings of a curve from the base of her spine that stretched the grey dress over her arse.

Her chest was flat. It was, and had always been, her eyes (that he later learnt had mascara applied) that produced a high colour in his cheeks when she looked straight at him. Thankfully, it went unnoticed by his mates still taking the piss out of his footwear.

"Hi Jane, sorry to keep you," said Eddie, sipping his coffee. "How are you?"

"I'm good, thanks. So busy night?"

"Yea, all small stuff, really busy till midnight then three more shouts at exactly two-hour intervals until six in the morning. It was as if someone has a grudge about us sleeping while on duty."

"I'm sure there are such people," Jane said.

"Most night workers do work the whole night." He was about to ask what he should do if there were no calls, run the Watch around the drill yard all night but didn't, he knew Jane was on his side.

"Hmmm, anyway after work, I popped over to see my dad."

"How is he?" She asked.

"Same ol same ol."

She smiled to herself, knowing Eddie was mimicking his father's over used phrase. "Good that's why I phoned."

"About my dad?" Eddie wasn't expecting this. "What's the matter?"

"Nothing. I thought of taking Ray to the cemetery tomorrow and wondered if you wanted to join us."

"No thanks."

"Are you—?"

"I went yesterday," he said, interrupting, "took flowers. And I'm busy tomorrow."

"What you doing?"

"Union meeting, the branch rep can't make it. I'd said I'd go for him. Take notes. But thanks," said Eddie.

"That's okay, you know I would always ask you."

"No, thanks for taking my dad," he paused.

"Eddie!"

Unable to fill the silence that followed, he said, "See you soon yea."

"Yeah okay Eddie, see ya."

He poured the last of the coffee into his mug, emptied the grouts into a small plastic bin he kept for that reason, washed the Moka pot and saucepan up and wiped down the kitchen worktop.

He was annoyed with himself for finishing the conversation so quickly. He asked her nothing. This woman who had been a part of his life for so long. From that first awkward conversation in the school youth club to their adolescent fumbling while babysitting and the consummation of their relationship before his first trip at sea, Jane had been his pole star.

He came home from that trip with a wooden sword from Fiji. It was elaborately carved with palms and her name. He kept it for three months aboard ship trying to imagine her reaction to the antipodean present. It was a Sunday before shops opened all day when he knocked on her door. She let him in with a muted joy.

Separation proved a fertile ground for their shyness to grow. The wooden sword bought on the far side of the world now seemed out of place and stupid on a dull English Sunday. Her coy thanks and her elder brother's snigger made him feel stupid. For privacy, they walked the estate.

Jane told him of college and Saturday cinema, he told her about San Francisco and Billy Graham's Philmore West. She brought him up to date with their old school friends and what they were doing, he told her about Boogey Street in Singapore where the beautiful women were in fact men.

Outside of her house at the end of the walk, Eddie felt downhearted. Jane was animated about her friends and seemed uninterested in his travels. In that moment, he told her it was over and walked away. The next time they met, five years later at a party, she was married.

Chapter 5

It was a beautiful spring day and although it was still mid-morning, the sun was warm and the air so cool and crisp, you could drink it. Ray had been waiting on the pavement outside his house when Jane arrived to pick him up. The road Ray lived on was always full with parked vehicles. The housing estates of yesteryear were never designed for today's two car families. She had phoned ahead for this very reason.

"Morning," said Jane as he slipped in beside her with an ease that belied his years. He wore a pale-yellow open neck shirt over a dark grey suit and brown Oxford brogues.

"Morning, sweetheart."

The cemetery was in the old village behind the local park. The village and housing estate being separate entities. Architectural harmony was not high on the agenda of post war planners but it did allow one to appreciate the villages and imagine the rural idylls before the working classes flowed out of east and south London like the Thames, flooding Essex and Kent with their distinct glottal stop.

"Do you still wear Dunhill for Men, Ray?"

"Yes, love."

"I remember buying you a bottle one Christmas."

"I know, love."

Jane parked under a tree, something Ray would never countenance. She retrieved the flowers from the back seat and they made their way through the rusted gates and the old drunken headstones covered in lichen to the far side and the newer plots.

As they approached Eve's grave arm in arm, she could feel Ray's pace quicken. Jane gave the flowers to Ray and as he bent to place them in the vase laying prone on the earthy site, she noticed the absence of any bouquet.

"Oi. Oi."

She turned around to see Jim. "Hallo, Jim."

Jim pointed in the direction of his house. "Shortcut, don't tell the kids. I tell them to stick to the roads."

"Why?"

"Well, you never know."

Jane loved Jim because you had to. How could you not love a man that seemed to love the world? Jim lived in a big house with a big family, drove a big car and had a big heart.

"Hallo Ray, how are ya, same ol same ol," he said with a chuckle as Ray started to answer, then smiled and carried on tidying the plot.

"I spoke to Eddie yesterday, said you had a busy Sunday night," said Jane.

"S'right," Jim replied, "and I had to go to this patio job I had lined up straight from work. Spent the day humping crazy paving around. I was cream crackered come last night. So Emma got three quiet nights heh heh."

Her smile was her only acknowledgment of the sexual innuendo. "What's Eddie like at the mo?" she asked.

"Whad ya mean?"

"On the station, does he seem okay?"

"Yea fine, well a bit subdued since you know." He nodded towards Eve's headstone, "but OK. Still giving us the run around and still as—"

Jane knew Jim was searching for a word not in his usual vocabulary. "Pretentious?"

"Yea that's it," said Jim, laughing, "pretentious." He was gonna use that one when the next opportunity presented itself.

"You know him, Jane."

"Well, he does do pretentious so well, Jim."

Jim smiled. "Anyway, better be off before the kids catch me, see ya Jane, see ya Ray."

This ended their polite repartee and in all the years of friendship, a conversation had never progressed any further. Eve's grave had the advantage of a bench close by. Jane sat down and allowed Ray some time with his wife. He stood with a hand on the headstone now in silent communion.

Sitting in the warm sun, she wondered what he was saying. Was he apologising for wasted years, could he have been more what, receptive, more companionable. In the couple of years that she and Eddie had been school sweethearts, she had spent a lot of time at their house. Eddie, of course, was the main reason but Eve fascinated her.

She spoke to Jane as a peer, filling her with information, gossip and advice. She remembered to this day the occasion a disgruntled Eddie wanted to go play football with his mates instead of spending time with her.

"Go, go," said Eve, "we are fine here without you, are we not Jane?" And she was. She observed the family dynamic in the Hart household. They say opposites attract, therefore Ray and Eve must have been the perfect match. Eve, so warm, so open and chatty. She was an implacable reader. Books lay around the living room, some open face down, others with the dust jacket as a book mark. The glass coffee table was covered in cup rings, the ash trays were full. Her coat flung over the back of a chair.

Eve always wanted to know about Jane's week and asked about her family. She lent Jane books, nudged her in the ribs and winked, saying, "a bit saucy that one."

Ray managed an ambient temperature. He was a polite and unobtrusive partner. When at home, he would welcome Jane at the front door with a chilly smile and a glance at her shoes, which Jane knew was meant for her to take them off.

Ray read the newspaper and when he finished it, he would fold it neatly and place it methodically in the magazine rack. He wiped the glass coffee table and emptied the ashtrays. He took the coat from over the chair and hung it under the stairs while Eve laughed and smoked.

Now, she mused, the house they had shared was neat and clean and as cool as Ray's smile. They walked back to the car arm in arm. "How's that girl of yours, Jane?"

"Well and studying sociology at Reading."

"Another bloody Marxist.

Oh, for God's sake!

I was joking, love."

"No Ray, look at the car, it's covered in bird poo."

Chapter 6

Sam stood in the kitchen, trying to hide his nervousness. This was his first day. A week earlier, he had left training school as top recruit in his squad, accompanied by the unnerving sentence from his instructor.

"Well done and for your sins, you're going to Red Watch, Langden. Good luck, you'll need it."

"I'm the mess manager," said Ken, leaning on the central worktop. In front of him was a battered ledger, open, a biscuit tin with its lid off that seemed to be full of shop receipts, a fiver and the stub of a chinagraph pencil.

"You will join the mess club, it's a closed shop on this Watch. Eight quid, please."

"Er, I'm sorry, what now and what for?" asked Sam. He had been told to stick up for himself.

"What for!" Exclaimed Ken, looking over his readers.

"You're messing, that's what for. Eight quid gets you stand easy and lunch on days and an evening meal and breakfast on nights plus all the tea and coffee you can drink, now that's what I call a fucking good deal and yes now or within the hour."

Ken took a pen from the breast pocket of his shirt. "Name?"

"Sam, Sam Brown."

"Like the belt."

Sam thought Ken might be older than his dad. "No, it's Brown without the e," he said.

Ken pondered the information.

"Anyway, the mess manager is the most important bloke on the watch after the officers. So listen to me and you won't go far wrong. Now go and get the eight spondoolies."

He was passing the watch room when out stepped Luke. Luke had been the last recruit to join Red Watch three years ago and had been longing for this day when the mantle of junior buck passed on to someone else.

"Allo sprog," he said. God it felt good.

"Morning," said Sam.

"Where you going?"

"To get some money, for the mess manager."

"Oh, don't take any notice of him. Where's your fire gear?"

"In my car."

"In your car! Ain't no fucking good in your car. Better get it and put it in the second bay, you'll probably be on the pump today."

"Ok sure. I'm Sam, by the way."

"I know," said Luke, before walking away. "I'm Luke," he said over his shoulder.

Sam got his new fire gear out of the boot of his car. His fire boots were already inside his leggings. His tunic, he slung over his shoulder and in the crook of his arm, he carried his helmet upside down with his fire gloves inside. He placed his gear in the empty second bay roughly where he reckoned the rear cab doors would be.

"What you doing?" asked Perry, who was casually walking with his fire gear to the ALP in bay three.

"I'm putting my fire gear where Luke told me."

"Take no notice of him," said Perry. "The Sub will tell you what you're riding. Put it under the watch room window for now."

Sam picked up his fire gear. "I'm Sam," he said but Perry had already disappeared around the front of the aerial ladder platform. Sam went back to the mess room and offered Ken a tenner. Ken took the note with a seriousness that suggested he was receiving reparation from a child who had wronged him and needed to be taught a lesson.

"I'll give you the change later," and nodded towards the tray of tea.

"That's the last you'll see of that two quid," said Adam, sitting at the mess table with Jim. "I'm Adam, this is Jim, welcome to the Red."

"I'm Sam."

"Yea, we know. Ready to go?"

"Well, I've put my fire gear under the watch room window in the bay."

"Who told you to do that?"

28

"Perry."

"Take no notice of him. Someone could fall over it there. Put it at the back of the bay by the high-pressure hose. In the watch room is the rider's board that will tell you what lorry you're on each tour. But as it's your first day, you best wait until the Sub gets back. He'll tell you where he wants you today."

Sam put his tea down and moved his fire gear. Coming back to the mess room, he asked Adam where the lorries were. With that phrase, he felt like an old hand already. The instructor at training school would never countenance such terminology. Appliances, they are fucking appliances.

"They are on a shout," said Adam.

"So that's a Blue Watch shout?" asked Sam.

"Yea went out about eight thirty."

"There doesn't seem to be many people here," said Sam.

"Well, the Blue Watch that weren't on the shout have gone home and the rest of our watch are on the fire call. We come in early and ride for someone on the off going watch so they can get an early shoot. You'll get the hang of it."

With that two pumping appliances swung into the yard and pulled up at the back of bays one and two. Sam jumped up, keen to take over from the night watch.

"Sit down, sit down. Eddie will want to talk to you first before you do anything."

Eddie Hart walked into the mess room with leading fire-fighter Chris Everett whose real name was Alec. They were deep in conversation but Eddie broke off to say a general good morning to which there came a general reply. The room was filling with other members of the watch who had been on the shout. Picking up a mug of tea, Eddie turned and said to no one in particular.

"The pump needs derving up."

A fire appliance with less than three quarters of a tank was deemed to be empty.

"Ah, Sam, isn't it?"

"Yes, sir," replied Sam, jumping to his feet and spilling some tea on the table in the process.

"Hallo, I'm Eddie Hart, the Sub Officer on Red. The Station Officer is off sick this tour, so you've got me."

"Heaven help us," said someone from the melee around the tea tray. Eddie ignored the comment.

"The office is at the far end of this corridor," said Eddie, pointing. "Give me five minutes, finish your tea then come down and don't call me sir."

Eddie turned to the room, "don't forget to sign for your BA sets, lads," and with that he walked out of the mess room to the office.

"First clean that tea up," said Luke.

"Whey!" Came a chorus of derision from the watch who were now mostly sitting around the mess table.

"What! He's gotta learn," said Luke, leaning back, one arm draped over the back of his chair, the other holding his mug.

"Yep and who better to learn from than Mr Sprog Duntsford," said leading fire-fighter John Mullins, not looking up from his paper.

"I ain't a sprog anymore that title has now been passed on," said a puffed up Luke with a small flourish of the hand towards Sam.

Harry Samuels was one of the older Watch members. He had an easy-going manner and insouciant charm. Harry had been on the Blue Watch shout but looked like he had just stepped out of makeup ready for a film shoot advertising the latest cologne. Harry was known as Harryoo because he was terrible with names. He was sitting next to Sam but until now had been in conversation with Billy Butler on his other side.

"You're," he paused.

"Sam," said Sam.

"Sam, if you need any advice, don't be afraid to ask," and he pointed to the remainder of the watch as they all looked on, "but if you're having trouble sleeping at night then, quietly mind," he said, raising a finger, "you don't want to wake the rest of us, go and talk to Luke who will be in his stinking pit wanking over his car mags. There's nothing that bell end can't tell you about a big end. Ain't that that right, senior sprog?"

"Least I can remember what my bell end is for," said Luke, who was not in the least worried about Harry's piss taking. What did concern him, though he would never show it, was the term senior sprog. That was a moniker that could stick. Sam smiled, not knowing what to say.

He got up now the five minutes had passed. "Er, what should I call him?" He asked no one in particular.

He looked from one to the other as they said, "Sub Officer, Guvnor, Subo, Boss, Leon." The last brought a laugh around the table.

"Thanks," he said, trying to hide the sarcasm in his voice. He put the dirty mug on the tea tray that sat on the counter separating the mess from the kitchen. Ken, still in the kitchen and chatting to Gretchen the cook, looked over his readers.

"Fuck sake," he said, "recruits."

Chris Everett walked out of the mess with Sam as Luke shouted sarcastically, "I'll clean up your spilt tea."

"I'm Chris, one of the leading fire-fighters." Sam knew this from the rank marking on his epaulettes but remained silent. "I'm in charge of the water tender this tour and Eddie will probably put you on that machine with me. After you've had your chat with him, come and find me, I'll be in the watch room and call him Sub, OK."

"Thanks."

"Call him Sub for a few tours then when the time is right, you can call him Eddie."

"How will I know?" asked Sam.

"You will," said Chris, walking away.

Eddie sat in the Station Officers' room. It was a better space than his room for these informal chats and introductions. He liked having a new recruit join them, new blood and all that but it always changed the dynamic of the Watch usually for the good but if the new boy didn't fit in, then the negative vibe could be problematic.

The day ahead should be routine, he thought. No big drills with other stations, no planned visits to the BA chamber at Divisional HQ, no parties of school kids visiting. Perfect day to introduce someone new to the watch and get him settled.

Eddie couldn't decide if he was pleased or disappointed that the Red never got a female recruit. He had championed the right of women to peruse a career in the Service and it pleased him to know that of the four women in this latest squad, three had graduated.

If he was really honest with himself though, he knew a female on the watch would present a unique challenge for him. One that he was sure he wasn't prepared for. His mind drifted back a couple of weeks, before he had been told they were getting Sam and there was the distinct possibility that a female recruit could be sent to the Red.

He realised he had not worked with women throughout his working life. From his days at sea to the factories and building sites and oil refineries, his working companions were always male. Sure women were present in offices, etc. but never alongside him as such.

He knew with a female fire-fighter, the Watch would scrutinise his every action and word, taking every opportunity to piss take and undermine his politically correct stance, mostly just for the fun of it but also to score points against him in an argument they normally lost.

There was a knock on the door. "Come in," said Eddie. "Sit down, Sam."

The chair Eddie gestured to had its back to the wall and was at right angles to the station officer's desk. Sam picked up the chair and repositioned it, allowing him to sit directly opposite Eddie in a formal pose. Eddie leaned forward and stretched out his hand. "Welcome to Red Watch, Sam."

"Thank you, Sub."

Eddie looked at the paper work in front of him and read aloud. "Top recruit, equal competency in theory and its practical application. Improvement in physical strength recommended, not required at this time. Ff Brown has proved to be a popular and effective member of the squad. It is hoped that Ff Brown will have a long and successful career."

Eddie looked up. "Well, they've set you your first challenge."

"Excuse me," said Sam.

"Your first challenge, Red Watch, Langden."

"Oh yea, they said."

Eddie thought of pursuing Sam's remark but decided against it for their initial meeting. "Never mind," said Eddie and smiled. He closed the file. "How old are you, Sam?" Eddie knew this fact but needed to start the conversation somewhere.

"I'm twenty, Sub."

"And before this, job wise."

"Nothing, really."

"Nothing. Come on, tell me about yourself."

"I was reading History at Queen Mary's."

"And, why the fire service?"

"To save life, property and to render humanitarian services."

"Ok, that's the official line. Now, tell me why you really joined."

Sam collected his thoughts, glanced at the row of fire service manuals lined up along the shelf behind the Sub Officer, noticing volume six, practical fireman-ship was missing. He breathed in.

"I enjoyed it but my whole life had consisted of books and academic tests and little else. I had passed every exam I'd ever sat with comparative ease. I needed, and you have probably heard this many times before a new challenge. Men my age from previous generations were presented with suchlike challenges, whether they liked it or not and I felt like I needed it too. It wasn't a sudden decision to ditch university, I was gradually becoming disenchanted with my life and not understanding why.

"This need, lying dormant in me, was awakened one day when I witnessed a fire. I had left a lecture and was walking down the Mile End Road. I was contemplating what I'd been listening to when I looked up and saw the blue lights. They were outside a terrace of early 18th century townhouses. Smoke and flame was pouring out of two ground floor windows next to the front door. I joined the crowd to watch.

"There were four or five fire engines. Police had stopped the traffic. Fire-fighters were running out hose, some to the front door, and some down the street to a fire hydrant. Two were putting on breathing apparatus and being helped by two more. To me, it looked like organised chaos if that makes sense.

"I looked up at the building and to my astonishment, saw a woman and child leaning out of a second-floor window; luckily, a wind was taking the smoke away from them. It was obvious they were trapped. I had a mixture of deep fear for the mother and child and I hope you don't think this strange, excitement wondering how they would be saved.

"It was then I noticed in the middle of all this, a fire-fighter in a white helmet standing still and surveying the scene. It only lasted seconds, I guess but it was a defining moment for me. The officer then started shouting orders. Two fire-fighters hit the smoke and flame coming out of the ground floor with a jet.

"Four fire-fighters put a ladder up to the second floor while shouting to the woman not to do anything, they were coming. Two other fire-fighters played a spray of water over the ladder. Two fire-fighters in breathing apparatus went through the front door with more hose. A fire-fighter ran up the ladder and went into the bedroom, a second fire fighter climbed the ladder.

"The first guided the child on to the ladder and the second fire-fighter still on the ladder, patiently guided her step by step down the ladder. The first fire fighter got back on the ladder from the bedroom window and then guided the woman out of the window and down the ladder in the same manner. When they were both on the ground, the crowd cheered. That was it that was when I knew."

Eddie looked at Sam. He had asked recruits that question many times before. He recalled some of the answers.

"Felt like a change."

"Out of work."

"Dunno really."

"Have you ever contemplated a job with the News at Ten?" Eddie asked.

"I'm sorry," said Sam.

"It doesn't matter."

Then the emergency lights went on and seconds later, the bells went down. It was a fire call. Eddie stood, making his way quickly out of the office, he told Sam to follow him. As they reached the main lobby area at the foot of the stairs, members of the Watch were walking from the mess room to the appliance bay. Two walked down the stairs from the locker room. A voice over the tannoy said, "All three. Hospital."

Eddie walked into the watch room and took the call sheet from Chris. It said the automatic fire alarm had gone off in the mental health unit. It was a common occurrence. Eddie turned to speak to Sam and had to take a step back because Sam was so close.

"You got your fire gear?" Eddie asked.

"Yes Sub, in the bay by the," he quickly thought of all the places he had placed it earlier, "at the back of the bay."

"Good. Chris, he's with you."

"Sam," said Chris, "get on the back of the water tender, you are going on your first shout."

Sam ran to the back of the bay and picked up his fire gear. Looking up, he saw Ken fully dressed and holding open a rear door of the water tender's cab. As Sam ran up to him, Ken said, "The middle, you sit in the middle." Sam looked in the cab. Billy Butler, also fully dressed was sitting at the far side of the cab, looking back at him. Billy said nothing.

Sam threw his boots and leggings into the middle and climbed the three steps up, suddenly missing the top step, his foot was in mid-air as his shin slid down the aluminium step edge. "Fucking recruits," said Ken.

The diesel engine roared as they slipped out of the station and into a line of traffic. Sam was frantically trying to dress. At training school, they dressed before going on the drill yard, ready for what was expected of them.

This was completely unexpected, he thought the first day would be, well rather casual. Introductions, perhaps a tour of the station and keys to his locker. It had so far been like the fire on the Mile End Road, chaotic. The lorry swayed through the traffic. Sam leaned over to put an arm through his tunic, resting against Ken as he did it.

"Got enough room?"

"Sorry, Ken."

Billy Butler spoke for the first time. "Get dressed but don't panic. 99 times out of a 100 this is a false alarm but be ready just in case."

The three appliances arrived within minutes of one another at the front of ward seven. A man stood by the front door holding a large bunch of keys. Eddie, whose rescue pump had arrived first, was the only one to get out. The rest of his crew stayed on board. When the water tender stopped, Chris turned and said, "Come with me, Sam."

Sam looked at Ken. Ken looked back. Sam looked at Billy. Billy opened his door and got out, letting Sam get off. Sam ran next to Chris. As they joined Eddie, the male nurse was apologising. Sam did not catch the whole conversation. He thought the nurse said a man threw a chair, narrowly missing him and hitting a call point.

Eddie turned to Chris but didn't say anything, he didn't have to. Chris nodded. "Come with me, Sam," and to the man Chris said, "Better show me."

Eddie remained in the foyer while he waited. He radioed to his driver and asked him to send an informative message to control. Fire alarms should not actuate repeatedly without good cause and the reasons should be addressed and taken care of. Senior officers wanted action taken against repeat offenders in a bid to drive down unnecessary fire calls.

Eddie felt differently about the Ward 7. The patients on this ward with their mental health problems had to be considered. He always cut the nursing staff some slack.

"Will do, captain," came the reply over the personal radio Eddie had slung over his shoulder.

While he waited, Eddie looked at the art work on the walls. They were mainly prints. A Rothko, a Lawrence Alma Tadema and a water colour of the local Church probably done by a staff member or patient. Eddie stood in front of the Rothko and wondered what thought was given to these pieces of art.

It consisted of a large rectangle of black over a slightly smaller rectangle of orangey red. The back ground was orange. Did anyone consider that black menacing mass and the effect it could have on a patient with depression or anxiety? Perhaps he was overthinking it. His radio crackled.

"Eddie."

"Yea Chris, go ahead."

"We are all good here, you can send the stop."

"Thanks, Chris."

Adam was driving the rescue pump and also heard the message. "Usual, Eddie," he said.

"Yes mate, false alarm, etc."

The aerial ladder platform was already slipping out the gates as Chris and Sam joined Eddie outside the hospital ward.

"One day," said Chris.

"I'll get back to the station," said Eddie, "you going messing?"

"Yea," said Chris, "see you in a bit."

Sam got back on the water tender. He looked at Ken. "It was a false alarm," he said.

"Well, thank fuck for that," said Ken, "perhaps we can go shopping now."

"Where to?" Came the question from Jim in the front.

"Sainsbury's, please," said Ken.

Chris booked mobile and available over the main scheme radio. Billy Butler looked out the window. Ken reached into his tunic and pulled out a shopping list. Sam rubbed his sore shin, trying to keep the smile from his face.

Chapter 7

Eddie closed down home station over the main scheme radio system as they pulled into the yard. He got off the lorry and was walking through the main lobby when Clarence Siddall called him from his office.

It occupied a part of the station that was an extension to the original. The welcome addition consisted of the station commander's office, the fire prevention office and a small but well-equipped gym. Next to Clarence Siddall's office was the main entrance to the station though it was rarely used.

These double doors were always locked for security. In addition, the appliance bay doors looking onto Church Road opened only for fire calls and presented an unwelcoming austere front to its citizens. The back of the station was the reckless twin, especially in the summer months. It was open for business and pleased to help. It said come in and people did.

They wandered in through the gates and asked if they could have a quick peak at the fire engines. No one was ever refused. A friendly soul might say they had an uncle in the London fire service and enquired if he was known here. Enthusiasts would ask to take pictures of the lorries, knowing far more technical data about them than the fire-fighters. Mothers and fathers would hold children in their arms, endeavouring to enthuse their offspring with a sense of wonder.

Eddie crossed the main foyer to the ADO's office. "Morning, Clarence."

It irked Clarence Siddall that Eddie did not show deference to his rank. "Good morning, Sub Officer."

"Temporary Station Officer actually."

Clarence Siddall ignored the fact that while Station Officer Arthur Church was off, Eddie stepped up a rank. Clarence Siddall looked at his computer screen. "One minute, I just need to," he stopped in mid-sentence.

Eddie stood looking past the station commander at the wall behind him. It was covered in commemorative plaques and memorabilia given to the station since its inception in the sixties and at the centre was the certificate of commendation presented to fire-fighter Clarence Siddall for his part in the rescue of a young man stuck in mud in the Thames estuary while bait digging.

Eddie ran his tongue over his gum.

"I'm rather busy, Temporary Station Officer," he stressed the first syllable of Eddie's rank, "So I'll come straight to the point. I had Len Duff in here at the end of your last tour, complaining that the petty cash was out and the machines were filthy."

"How much?"

"Pardon?"

"How much was it out?"

"I can't recall but that's not the point."

"What machines were dirty?"

"The water tender, I believe."

"You believe."

"Yes, look I don't want to make a big thing about it but."

"Seems to me you are trying to make something of it."

"It's the thin end of the wedge. Keep on top of it."

"Is that it?"

"I want to see your recruit."

"He's still out, I'll send him in when he gets back."

Eddie turned and left the office before Clarence Siddall said another word. The water tender had arrived back at the station with the messing. Stand easy was taken at eleven o clock. Tradition was a cheese and onion sandwich and a mug of tea but food like pay and conditions had seen improvements over the years along with fire-fighter's expectations. Ken the mess manager, ever the traditionalist, had long conceded to baguettes filled with ham and pickle or tuna mayonnaise with sweet corn.

Perry Jackson and Billy Butler were in the kitchen, helping Ken and Gretchen butter the bread, grate cheese and make the huge pot of tea enough for the whole Watch. Sam Brown looked over the counter separating the kitchen from the mess room, taking in the scene.

Ken looked up. "Cheese, ham or tuna," he said.

"Oh er, not for me, thank you," said Sam. "I am trying to go vegan. Not as easy as I thought but I'm giving it a go."

Ken stopped filling baguettes and stared at Sam as if he had spoken Serbo-Croat. "Vegan. Fuckin vegan, are you Jewish or Muslim or summit?"

Perry Jackson and Billy Butler were smiling while they buttered. "It's a plant-based diet, no animal or dairy products."

Ken hadn't finished. "Stand easy is supposed to be a mid-morning break, that's all, a quick cheese and onion sarnie on plain sliced white bread washed down with a nice mug of Rosie Lee. These days I provide brown bread, baguettes, rolls all filled with the entire deli section of Sainsbury's and now he wants me to provide leaves and grass and, and." It was obvious that Ken's knowledge of the vegan diet was not that extensive so he finished with what he did know about. "Fuckin recruits," he said.

"Sam, station commander wants to see you," said Eddie as he came into the mess room. "You've seen his office right. He won't keep you long so reciprocate accordingly."

Harryoo walked past.

"Go on son, cut along, mustn't keep the Guvnor waiting."

Harryoo picked up the tray of tea and placed it on the mess table. He returned to the counter and took a ham baguette. Eddie was about to take his cheese roll when the bells went down.

Chapter 8

The promenade at Chalkwell ran alongside the Thames estuary for what Eddie assumed must be five miles to Shoeburyness. The tarmacadam path with its slight camber to the river was hemmed by a low sea wall on one side and a bank of grass, rocks and succulents on the other.

Soon to follow were the Arches. These vaulted caverns, once used by the local fishermen to store equipment were now bohemian eateries that nestled on the opposite side of the road to the river at Westcliff on Sea. He parked in the road at Chalkwell train station and by the time he had reached the restaurants, he thought of stopping for a drink as he used to, when he worked at Westcliff.

A small one pump station that the Chief Fire Officer knew to be an unnecessary drain on his budget and which took him some years to convince the wealthy business community that it's closure would in no way deplete their fire cover. The station where he and Clarence Siddall had worked together. Fire-fighters on the same watch.

Eddie strolled the prom, enjoying the evening air. It had been a busy day. The morning's fire calls amounted to nothing and the new recruit, though not seeing any flames, had got a flavour for going out the doors. This meant Sam never got to speak to Clarence Siddall, who was gone by lunchtime.

Eddie decided against a drink and carried on to the pier. It was low tide, the timber structure pushed out over the mudflats like a thirsty tree root to the constant river over a mile out. The low sun was London bound. The angled light contrasted the rich grey clag and black silent tide pools, where Lapwing, Godwit and Dunlin had feasted over the winter.

The same foul-smelling ooze that he and Clarence Siddall had walked, crawled and slid over with ladder, salvage sheet and sand lance to free the young bait digger from the quick sand holding him fast as the tide slipped silently in like an errant lover returning home to bed.

He remembered a childhood here with his mother. The long summer evenings, deckchairs and sandwiches and Rossi's ice cream cones that he would lick diligently, never allowing the cream melt to run over his hands. Where was his father, Eddie couldn't recall. At work probably. He would watch the ships tramp up and down the river and imagine the destination of cargoes, ocean bound. His mother pretended to know the terminus of all the vessels and would enchant him with exotic place names.

"That white one is bound for Lisbon all the white ships go to Portugal and blue ones to Madagascar."

"The red one?" Eddie would ask.

"Ah now red ones can be tricky, devious. Montevideo or Cape Town. Can't make out the flag, can you?"

"No, Mum."

"Likely to be a pirate then," she would say, keeping a straight face. Later, she would encourage him to look up the ports on his globe.

They would sit on a bench and while he concentrated on his ice cream, Eve would watch the promenades. Her gaze would follow young couples passing hand in hand, silent or laughing, the girl wearing her man's jacket over her shoulders for warmth. He then discreetly sliding his hand around her waist, pulling her close, smelling her hair.

Eve watched until a thought interrupted her reverie, a thought that creased her brow. She would reach into her hand bag to retrieve her cigarettes and the small petrol lighter that she would repeatedly flick because the flint had worn low. A man might stop to offer her a light, which she accepted with polite charm. Eddie noticed how the man's gaze lingered a few seconds before he turned to Eddie, smiled and went his way.

There were times when they brought Peter who lived next door, he was two years younger than Eddie, quiet and ineffectual. A sweet child, Eve would say of him and showed him the kindness and love a younger son would expect. It was not a problem for Eddie to share his mother's affection. She always made it clear to him that he was number one, demonstrating it when at home singing along to records while cooking Sunday lunch.

He could still recall kneeling in front of the radiogram with record sleeves strewn about him while he chose her favourite tracks and his mother turning around from the sink to hold his gaze through the door while singing the lyrics directly to him.

"Sentimental syrup," she would say but Eddie knew she meant it.

As Eddie walked alongside the river, the river that ran through his life, these thoughts of work and childhood commingled. It troubled him that on this beautiful evening, thoughts about work were winning the battle in his head.

Clarence Siddall was the trouble. It was clear he had taken against the Red Watch and Eddie since taking charge of Langden fire station. What was lacking in clarity was the reason for his disfavour. When they worked at Westcliff, Eddie thought they got on fine. They would spend the quieter evenings playing snooker and table tennis.

They would sit looking out of the first-floor games room and watch the late commuters leaving the railway station, close enough to witness their dismay upon seeing the empty taxi rank. Clarence Siddall had even confided in him about his anger at being overlooked in favour of his younger sister.

"I lacked business acumen, my father said, your sister has foresight, and the company needs someone with that ability at the helm."

Clarence Siddall was bitter but why with me, thought Eddie. He was getting close to the pier and thought of turning but didn't. What's more, he had kept Clarence Siddall's foolishness when a fire-fighter secret. Never breathed a word. Did he think I had told the Red Watch and they had taken against him, he considered, no surely not?

Maybe the secret was brewing a poison, perhaps to talk about it now would be the antidote. That was easier said than done. He had come to dislike Clarence Siddall. Management had revealed unworthy traits in him. He used his power on the weakest, despised the lower ranks that stood up to him and fawned over his bosses. Any redeeming feature he had when a fire-fighter had been subsumed in his desire for power and promotion.

Assume as he might, Eddie knew it would not be a chat that awaited the two of them but an angry confrontation. A shriek of laughter and the sound of a machine paying out a jackpot broke his train of thought. He looked at the penny arcades with their neon colours, garish against a darkening sky. Surprised at how far he had walked, he turned and headed back to his car.

Chapter 9

With the closure of Westcliff fire station, the careers of Eddie Hart and Clarence Siddall took different paths. Eddie had been transferred to Tilbury. A relatively quiet station where the main risk was Tilbury docks. It was his first choice because of the fire tugs that they would man for any incident on the river. It was during his time at Tilbury that Eddie took and passed all the fire service exams to Station Officer level.

The idea of studying for three years was not foremost in his mind when he arrived at Tilbury but Albert Goodman, the Sub in charge of White Watch; a man who prided himself on recognising potential, had been the catalyst that drove Eddie back to study.

Eddie's only concern when told of his transfer to Tilbury was the moniker applied to the White Watch. The pipe and slipper Watch. Albert Goodman was the avuncular leader of a group of smoke eaters. Fire-fighters tend to find their way to the busy or quiet stations as a matter of personal choice. The men on White Watch had gravitated to Albert for their own well-judged reasons.

Young fire-fighters on Albert's watch were drilled regularly and listened to lectures on every night shift. They kept the appliances immaculate. If the volleyball session was interrupted by a fire call, it was not continued upon return to the station, it was lost. Albert Goodman would brook no horseplay or pranks. He considered practical jokes to be a cruelty.

This meant they escaped at the earliest opportunity to other watches to be replaced by the older hand whom Albert had the respect to leave alone, providing all routines were completed as required and of course they were. He stopped checking. The watch settled into comfortable habits. They enjoyed cooking and sharing recipes.

There was a book club, loosely formed, that centred on a spare locker full of read and waiting to be read. The TV showed documentaries. Conversation was interesting, arguments picked apart and considered and words, words that Eddie loved so much, used without a stupid 'ooh swallowed a fucking dictionary' type comment.

For the first few months, Eddie busied himself with all that was new and different from his old station. He laughed when blokes at change of shift asked if he enjoyed his liquidised dinners with a glass of Sanatogen. He took it in good part when opening his locker and a wad of incontinent pads fell out. But as the months became a year, Eddie had to admit to himself how much he enjoyed being part of the watch.

His early misgivings, the constant piss taking were nothing compared to the culinary delights and good conversation he now enjoyed and when the bells did go down, he admired how an incident was dealt with such untroubled ease and then there was Albert Goodman.

Albert was fifty. His ramrod back and square shoulders pulled his shirt tight over a small paunch. His hair was grey and thinning. A tattoo on one forearm gave a clue to the younger Albert Goodman. The torso of a half-naked women sat above four aces. In front of the four aces were dice and a bottle. The inky vignette was enclosed in a horse shoe and underneath were two words, Man's ruin.

Albert, like Eddie, had served in the Merchant navy for twelve years, rising to the rank of Master at Arms. The ship's policeman. When Eddie mentioned one day in the mess of his time at sea, Albert looked up from the standing orders he was reading and gave the slightest nod of affirmation. The conversation Albert wanted to have immediately with Eddie would wait for the opportune moment when they were alone.

Ex seamen enjoyed swinging the lamp. Stories of exotic women in far-flung ports and a list of ships that one had sailed on. These esoteric conversations could never have been explained or enjoyed as much with someone inexperienced in such a life. It was the same with fire-fighters talking of fires they had been in.

They knew civilians had little or no comprehension of what it's like to crawl through a smoke-filled building not seeing a thing, feeling around and under furniture, trying desperately to locate a body while hoping from all the confused messages that everyone had already escaped.

Stories shared of broiling seas and raging fires. The link between the two professions had been long established. Firemen originally worked in and lived on the fire station. It was considered wise by the powers that be to employ ex seamen as they were used to living in close quarters with their fellow man. Hence the coalescence of borrowed terminology, the Watch, the mess, stand easy.

So a bond formed between the two men and although Eddie by now was no longer a recruit, Albert became his mentor. When they returned from a shout, Albert made a point of asking Eddie what he had learnt. Learn something from every shout son, no matter how small or seemingly inconsequential, piece by piece, build your experience.

One slow evening after dinner, the two remained in the mess room while the others drifted off to their various pass times. Albert had been telling Eddie of one particular voyage when having just been made Master at Arms, he came across a fight involving three of the crew.

It was a hot night off the Mexican coast the sea flat calm. Two men were trying to throw another overboard. Albert rushed to the fracas, shouting at them to stop.

"I nearly went over myself," said Albert, "my god they were determined. If it hadn't been for a couple of officers hearing the row, I would have been in trouble. Turns out the guy was a thief. Men, as you know when living together will tolerate most things but not that."

"Were they charged?"

"Of course, all three."

"What was the outcome?"

"Made 'em walk the plank," said Albert, laughing, pleased how the joke had popped into his head. "You never tried for promotion, Eddie?"

"No, not for me."

"Why not?"

Eddie shrugged, "not the type."

"Not what type?" asked Albert.

"The type to laud it over others. No offence, Albert."

"None taken."

"I have never wanted to be part of the system."

"And what system is that?" asked Albert, slipping off his shoes and placing his feet on a chair.

"You worked the passenger liners Albert, didn't you?"

Albert nodded.

"I done a few trips on them as well," continued Eddie. "My cabin was literally in the bowels of the ship. There was twelve to a cabin. We had a bunk a locker and a diddy box on the bulkhead by our bunk. As you went up the decks, the conditions improved. At the top of the ship was the captain in a suite of rooms all to himself. I always thought it a perfect example of the system."

"Did you ever consider what the captain had to do to get that suite of rooms and the responsibility that lay solely on his shoulders as opposed to what was expected of you?"

"Of course," said Eddie, he paused. "I just wanted a better cabin," he said, smiling.

"Look Eddie, I watch you with the rest of the watch. You have an easy way about you, you go about your work quietly and methodically but when you have something to say, it seems to carry weight even regarding the ordinary and every day. The old hands listen to you in a way they wouldn't with some of the other youngsters."

"Was the skipper on that liner a bad skipper in your opinion?"

"Not that I recall," said Eddie.

"You can't do enough for a good guvner, that's the saying eh. You could be that guvner Eddie, serving the public in a job you love." He watched Eddie taking it all in. "And," said Albert Goodman, "You get your own room."

Eddie remained at Tilbury for five years before his first promotion as a leading fire-fighter to Grays. On his last day at Tilbury, the goodbyes were light-hearted, plenty of backslapping, thumps on the arm and a chorus of fuck offs from most except for the Sub Officer.

He went into Albert Goodman's office, leaned across the desk and shook him by the hand. The tactile gesture was enough. It conveyed the recognition of tutor and pupil and how by chance, lives and careers could cross.

"Thanks, Albert."

"Good luck," said Albert, "and remember firm but fair."

Clarence Siddall went to the north of the county. It could have been a different brigade. A person could work thirty years and not meet colleagues from the north or south respectively. The travelling was a pain at first. Long hours behind the wheel, many stuck in traffic as the good people of Essex raced one another up and down the A12 and when they got it wrong, jammed this major artery.

He would listen to the local radio station. The frequent traffic reports giving him some idea as to how long he would be stuck. He would look around at the other drivers and wonder if they felt the same. A mile up the road perhaps could be various scenarios, two men out of their cars and arguing about right of way or worse people trapped with painful injuries or gone, more lives taken by this road, devil incarnate.

He wondered if the other motorists felt annoyed, if they were frustrated to the disruption to their day, if they were, maybe worse of all, bored. Clarence Siddall felt all three. Then he hated driving by the wreckage when the crews were still there.

Maybe try a tentative wave should one look up and see him or should he ignore them and hope he got passed without recognition. The former method carried the chance of a blank stare and no response, it tightened his gut. The latter would leave him with the not knowing. What if he had been noticed? He imagined the comments, "stuck-up cunt, prick."

After three months of this grind, he was lucky to find digs with a woman who rented a room to police and fire only. He would stay there for his tour of duty and after the two days two nights were over, take the drive down south to his bungalow in Thorpe Bay. Bought for him by his father when he was told his sister got the top job.

He had nearly thrown the keys back at his father. He wanted to shout, I want nothing from you, I'll make my own way in this world and prove you wrong. He didn't, he said thank you, looked at his sister, smiled and left his father's office.

Oh how glad he was he had kept the keys. Clarence Siddall loved his home. His property was on a tree lined street of quiet unassuming wealth. He made a point of never leaving or returning in uniform. He was one of them. A solicitor, a doctor, a company director. He imagined joining the yacht club but that would be revealing his profession. Then they would know of his modest income, assume he was a daddy's boy.

No, he kept himself to himself. Clarence Siddall purchased expensive luggage. He was the business man away for a few days, not a fire-fighter going on shift. In some ways, working in the north of the county was perfect. The chance of meeting a neighbour when dressed as a fire-fighter was negligible.

His world split in two. North and South. The South became the sunlit uplands of his life. Owning his own property gave Clarence Siddall disposable income. On his weekend's off, he would cruise the bars in Leigh. Each night always started with high expectations as he got ready at home. He imagined walking in, noticing the turning heads as he made his way to the bar.

Ordering a gin and tonic, he would perch on a bar stool, nonchalantly playing with the twizzle stick in his drink while surveying the room. He would check his snide Rolex as if waiting for someone. Then the inevitable would happen. A beautiful woman would come to the bar, standing next to him she would smile, he smiled back. She couldn't get the attention of the bar staff.

"Busy night," he would say. "Always the same in this place, never enough people serving."

Joe, a young man pulling a pint, looked round and Clarence Siddall motioned with his eyes to the beauty next to him.

"Thanks."

With her drinks, she would return to her female group. He watched as the others looked his way. She explaining how she was served. As the evening wore on, she would return, a longer conversation would take place, he would make her laugh, tell her where he lived then exchange numbers. That's what he imagined.

Usually, he took up an unobtrusive place from where he could enjoy watching an evening unfold. He preferred Friday nights. Saturday was for couples. Friday saw the groups of men and women out with mates, all dressed to kill, posing, looking, joking and laughing.

Clarence Siddall new laughter was key but it was so difficult to enter into a conversation and make light of something in those crucial first minutes. Far easier in a group where one is already joking peacock style, throwing out casual remarks to passing girls.

Try that on your own and you would look weird, unnerving. There was the occasional stilted chat after a few drinks but when the smart shirt and fake watch failed to impress, he could tell she wanted to reverse out of the dull cul de sac back to fun city.

That was until he walked into his favourite joint on Broadway one Friday night. There at the bar was a group of off duty fire-fighters from Leigh. The car crash scenario on the A12 flashed through his mind, then the one man who turned from the group and noticed him come through the doors, smiled.

"Clarence Siddall, how are ya?" It was Leo Grant. They had been at training school together and since graduating, their paths rarely crossed. Leo was already a Sub Officer and working at HQ. Leo's father had been a Chief Officer in Norfolk and a lot was expected of Leo. Thus far, he had not disappointed.

He had passed all the statutory exams and was a member of the institute of fire engineers. Leo Grant had an air of eternal optimism and a library full of anecdotes. Howard Carter's retelling of his discovery of the tomb of Tutankhamun would pale in comparison with Leo Grants exploits over a dull weekend in Essex.

He would enter a room with a greeting to all and start speaking, addressing everyone while addressing no one in particular. It was for this reason mainly that he had acquired the nick name, unknown to him, of Thrush, because he was an irritating cunt. His heart was in the right place.

"Everyone, this is Clarence Siddall, same squad."

A few said hello, some nodded, everyone carried on with their conversations.

"What brings you to this neck of the woods, I thought you went north after Westcliff, haven't seen you in here before, oh I remember now you have a place in Thorpe Bay, very nice, you on your own or are you meeting someone?"

As the Proustian sentence gathered pace, Clarence Siddall considered remaining silent and allow Leo to answer all the questions himself.

He interjected. "I'm meeting a friend," he lied.

"A friend, yea I bet, you old dog. Well until she arrives, join us for a drink, in fact, have this one, I'm already behind, haven't touched it."

He thrust a bottle into the hands of Clarence Siddall who rarely drank beer but was already feeling overwhelmed.

"I'm here with my old watch, they do this now and again and I got wind of tonight's little drink up so I thought I'd pop along for old time sake."

Clarence Siddall looked at the group of young men and one woman, chatting laughing, eyeing the room. The one thing they had in common it seemed to him was they were glad he had turned up and taken Leo off their hands. Clarence Siddall was more than happy to oblige. Now as Leo prattled on, he could smile and nod his head agreeing with his friend, just one of his friends and when he laughed, he radiated fun.

Could this be the night? After two more beers, Clarence Siddall ordered a gin and tonic. "Drowning your sorrows?" asked Leo Grant.

"Pardon?"

"She's not coming by the look of it. Oh, it was only if she could get away from her old man."

"No, no, I—"

"I'm only joking. Look, meeting you here may be fortuitous for us both. Have you ever thought of day work only I've been charged with finding someone for such a role?"

"Why, I—"

"There is a job coming up in Staff at the Funny Farm. We could work together, be a laugh. I should be able to pull a few strings and get you transferred ASAP. You have your exams, don't you, of course you do. What say you, think it over but not for too long, these jobs are gold dust for bods wanting to climb the greasy pole anyway your round methinks and if I'm not mistaken, those two lovelies over there have been staring this way awhile now. Get 'em in and we'll saunter over."

So Clarence Siddall transferred to HQ. The job came with his first promotion and an immediate temporary promotion to Sub Officer. Clarence Siddall never saw a great deal of Leo who had been given a special project that if went well, would enhance his career and that was exactly what Clarence Siddall needed. The chance to prove himself and to someone superior enough to mentor his own rise through the ranks.

Divisional Officer Gladstone was a bastard. He believed it to be a prerequisite of command and life's natural order. Some men were born to lead, some to follow. The career fire-fighter in his opinion was unruly. A lazy and feckless character whose ambition it was to do as little as possible.

"I remember going to work," he was relating a story to Clarence Siddall as they sat in his office. "I remember going to work at the start of a tour and asking a fireman (despite organising promotional days aimed at women, he was steadfast with the former title) what type of night he had had."

His eyes narrowed as he tapped the desk with his delicately manicured forefinger. "Do you know what he replied?"

"Well, I can imagine a few choice."

The DO cut across him, "Robbed 'em blind. Robbed 'em blind," he repeated. "The most important thing for this, this man, was that he had come to work for 15 hours and done nothing."

Clarence Siddall shook his head, hoping it reflected his disgust at what he had just been told.

"Not a fire prevention inspection, not a talk to a local group, not any training or self-study, no he was proud that the tax payer had paid him to do nothing."

"Of course," he continued, "I blame the Watch officers, weak and happy with the path of least resistance. Don't become one of those Sub Officer. Don't be ineffectual. Rule!" He banged the desk, "Lead! We must show the Chief Fire Officer that the tail does not wag this dog. Take my advice, Sub Officer and you will go far."

"I will, Sir. I most certainly will," said Clarence Siddall.

Chapter 10

"I've restocked the shelves, washed the basins and cleaned the floor, can I go now?"

Jane turned from gazing out on to the high street, her reverie broken by the girl's plaintiff whine. "Did you get my milk?" Jane asked her apprentice.

The girl let out a sigh and rolled her eyes. She wasn't paid to run errands and skivvy, she wanted to learn to cut hair and dye hair and create new styles so she could open her own salon in Chelsea and coiffure the rich and famous. She would employ a bevy of the trendiest boys and girls and only cut and style a select few who could afford Chantal (that was the name she had long contemplated for herself).

"No," she said.

Jane looked at Mary. Was she, Jane thought, looking into a mirror of the past? Did she, Jane Hobson, lack any sense of work ethic at Mary's age, until life bit her on the arse, leaving its teeth marks like a slave's branding. We are working class, she mused.

We work and work for so long until we finally stop working and feel guilty that we no longer work anymore. She should tell Mary to fuck off with a rucksack and have fun instead of cleaning her shop for the next year or two before Mary decided hairdressing was not for her anyway.

"It's OK. I'll get it, you run along."

"Night, Jane."

"Night, Mary."

Jane looked around her newly refurbished shop. She pushed a chair in line with the other three. Pleased with her design. Four black chairs in front of four individual black work stations looked good on the Brazilian cherry laminate floor. The walls white and unadorned in contrast to the black shelving in the window lined with product. She worried if it looked austere and hoped in equal measure that it would encourage men into her domain.

Men? They, whoever they were, said women were complex creatures. Most of the men she knew were like a thousand-piece jigsaw with a bit missing. She wondered what Eve would have made of her metaphor.

Her father, an open and loving man who constantly grabbed Mum, nuzzling her neck, slapping her arse and when he thought the kids weren't looking, trying to touch her up. It wasn't that Mum never liked his attention and his hands on her; it was the other women he had his hands on also that dampened her enthusiasm for her husband's ardour. His bar staff never stayed. A neighbour nearby became the object of his desire until the husband threatened him.

"Lascivious," Eve Hart had called him.

"What can I get you sir, of course and for the lovely lady?"

Her mother's broad spectrum of feelings started with jealousy in the early years, lingered a while in anger before festering in disgust. When she arrived at tiredness, she left her husband and sued for divorce. Her share of equity in their business would be enough to start again. She took the kids but never denied him access to the children he truly loved.

Eve would go with Jane to the pub and stand at the bar with a drink while Jane and her father talked. Eve attracted men with her easy open manner but if by chance, they over stepped the mark then instantly the smile would drop from her face and her rebuke like a stiletto in the hands of an assassin found its mark. Jane always thought her father was scared by Eve.

The recognition that her father was a lecher pained her as much as it did her mother. So when Jane married Neville Hobson, it was with some trepidation that was quickly proved to be unfounded, for Neville had the libido of a frozen chicken. Jane was amazed they had a daughter and when she was born, it was as if Neville had fulfilled his side of the marital contract and could now concentrate on his judo, cycling and weekend orienteering.

Neville was a good man. He was good with money, he rarely drank, had an even temper, doted on his daughter and loved his wife. Nev was the exception to the rule, her oasis of calm. Jane's dad thought he was a wanker. *Another weekend getting lost in a field, Neville?* Was a favourite line of his when he popped in for tea.

Nev could have twatted Jane's dad so quickly that he would have only known about it as he came round but Nev was a good man and it was his wife's father. So Nev smiled and said yea. Jane wished her husband would twat her father just once.

"Why doesn't Dad twat granddad?" asked her daughter.

"Because your dad is a good man," Jane replied.

Then there was Eddie. The other man in or on the periphery of her life. She never really knew. Eddie Hart, half inch shy of six foot, slim and muscled in a manner that didn't offend. He could pass as Italian with his jet-black hair though it lacked the Mediterranean lustre.

She often witnessed a woman's hand raise in reflex, wanting to touch it and in that moment's hesitation and wayward glance, hope her intention had not been revealed. Eddie knew, could intuit a misjudged movement, a colouring of the throat. His eyes reminded her of a young John Wayne, the nose not quite as long and the lips fuller, his ears with the less dominant attached lobes sat tight to his head, his neck hairless and lightly tanned.

Eddie prided himself on his appearance. He weighed himself every other day, making sure his body mass index was acceptable and he moisturised. Jane was sworn to secrecy. In some ways so like his father, in some ways completely different. He would have his haircut every three weeks. She knew because she cut it. He would arrive after closing.

She would shut the blinds and get out her electric razors and scissors and before starting, Jane would stand behind him, look in the mirror and run her fingers through his hair in a pretence of professionalism. Occasionally, he would smell of smoke.

"Sorry, I rushed to get here." He would say.

"S'OK, tell me about your day," and he would. The one person outside the job he could talk to. Not so much the fire calls, more the day to day things that management involved.

Jane placed the day's takings in the safe in her office cum cleaner's cupboard, locked it then tried the back door, turning off lights as she went, her train of thought unbroken. Lately, Eddie had stopped talking. It had been, what, ten months since the accident and he showed no sign of improvement. A light had been turned off in one of the rooms in Eddie's life and he seemed afraid of the darkness therein.

His general demeanour was the same as anyone mourning loss. The shallow happiness in polite society, the smile of gratitude to anyone commiserating with him but Jane felt the change in him to be unnatural. His friends, what few there were, and his colleagues seemed prepared to give him more time. Jane knew he needed help.

Trying to talk to his father would be like talking to Eddie himself, useless. Jane saw grief from time to time when women came in the shop, having been widowed. She had watched during the repeated appointments how the women had come to terms with their loss and how they moved on. The comfort of their memories providing buoyancy.

There was something weighing Eddie down, a pressure smothering times transitioning arc. She remembered his inscrutable manner during the funeral and wake. The inability to cry in marked contrast with his father even when one of his mother's friends, a local singer stood in front of the congregation and sang her favourite song. This healthy beautiful man was flat lining. Jane had to get him to talk.

She took a last look around her salon before stepping out the front door, locking it and crossing the road to the mini mart for a carton of milk.

Chapter 11

It was that time again. A year had passed since Ken had last been asked to be the mess manager of Red Watch and he wanted the formality of their endorsement for another twelve months. Ken also wanted to play hard to get. If they felt like a change, someone with new ideas maybe, he wouldn't stand in their way was his opening gambit.

He sat at the mess table, waiting for the Watch's pleas and gratitude. He gazed down at his outstretched arm, his fingers beating a silent tattoo, lips pursed and brow knitted. Lff John Mullins spoke first.

"Perhaps it is time another member of the watch took on the responsibility," he said.

Ken looked up, his fingers fell silent.

"I'll do it," said Harry Samuels, looking straight at Ken.

If there was such a thing as a Watch's collective smile, it happened then. "You sure," said Perry.

"Yea, Ken's done it for what, two years now," said Adam.

"A change is as good as a rest," chimed Chris.

"I'm fuckin sick of chips and rice anyway," said Jim.

"And the constant increases in the mess charges," said Luke.

"Well, fucking do it then, Samuels. I'm fed up feeding you fuckin ungrateful bunch of—"

The rest of Ken's sentence was drowned out in a chorus of whey heying laughter and hands slapping the table. Sam Brown watched with a barely contained glee at the humour of the situation but also not sure which way it would go. Ken sat there waiting for the noise to subside, feeling the love while being annoyed at getting caught.

"Fuck the lot of ya, I'm putting the messing up." More cheers.

Ken looked around the table. His eyes came to rest on the laughing Sam Brown who was looking around the table. His eyes came to rest on Ken. His laughter cooled to an embarrassed smile while Ken held his gaze. Jim noticed the silent interchange.

"Fucking recruits," Jim said, imitating the mess manager, "been here five fucking minutes and he thinks it alright to take the piss."

"Yea, put his mess up," said Adam, "all that vegan shit."

"Thinks it's the fucking Savoy," said Billy Butler.

Luke Dunstford just had to join in on this one. "Maybe he should do the mess managers job," he said, looking at Sam. "See how hard it is, wouldn't last five minutes."

Sam coloured but knew at this point in his career, silence was the better part of valour. He held up his hand in recognition at his faux pas. Then he changed his mind. "I'll do it, when like Ken, I'm at the end of my career."

Eddie was in the Station officers' room. He had put the phone down from Station Officer Arthur Church when the cheer went up from the mess room. *What's going on down there*, he thought. He walked in to a raucous room of men sitting around the mess table. He saw at once Ken sitting at the head of the table, fingers thrumming, staring at Sam and Sam, eyes cast down, red in the face and smiling. No one need say anything. He had witnessed this scene so many times before.

"Listen up you lot," said Eddie. "I've just got off the phone from the guvner. He will be sick another month. Sciatica. So, can we do the routines, please?"

"I'll get on with your fucking grub," said Ken, going back to his kitchen. Chairs scrapped, cups clattered on the aluminium tea tray.

"What was all that about?" Eddie asked John Mullins as the watch made their way out to the appliance bay.

"New boy showing a bit of backbone," said John Mullins.

Chapter 12

Eddie kept the two tones on as they made their way through the heavy morning traffic. He had wanted to sit down with the Watch and run through a few mundane things that occupied the day to day organisation of station life but the fire call had scuppered that. Upper Church was divided by a golden band of daffodils swaying gently in their perennial beauty.

The adrenaline rush created by a shout heightened the senses. His brain was being assaulted by colour and light, he pulled down the sun blind, he noticed kids watching, a postie pulling an elastic band from a clump of letters and dropping it on the pavement and trees coming into leaf like something almost being said[1]. *I'm going to a road traffic collision and thinking of a poem by Phillip Larkin,* he thought.

"You should read him, son," his mother would say. "*They fuck you up,*"[2a] she said as she put her coat on.

"Who?"

"*Your mum and dad,*"[2b] she replied, looking at him, her head performing a slight angled dip, eyebrows raised that broke into a knowing smile. "Tell Dad I'm down the library, bye."

Dad fucked me up with his absence, he thought.

He still had his number one uniform on under his fire gear. He pulled the yellow surcoat from the back of his seat and struggled to get an arm through as the sleeve of his tunic snagged the armhole, he was hot. Cars parted like the Red Sea, fully aware of the part they had to play in someone's emergency, he pulled a pair of latex gloves on as Jim slowed the lorry.

"Look at this twat," said Jim.

---

[1] *The Trees* by Phillip Larkin.
[2a b] *This Be The Verse* by Phillip Larkin.

In front, a Toyota Cherry blocked their way, the driver seemly oblivious to the world around him or her.

"Got his drum and base on max," said Eddie.

"The stupid cunt ain't listening to us," piped up Adam from the back.

Luke was sitting behind Eddie, "do you want me to get out guv and move that old shitter for him," he said, shouting, his head and shoulders hanging out of his opened window.

"No," said Eddie, "and get your head back inside, this ain't a horse box."

Two cars realised the situation and pulled their offside wheels up on to the central res, a third followed. As the rescue pump slipped past, Jim's hand gave a casual wave from the open window to the astute drivers.

Eddie looked down into car causing the obstruction. He first noticed the hands clasped to the wheel. Their skin a translucent tissue covering the swollen veins running up arms stick thin. The elderly man sat transfixed as the proverbial rabbit in the head lights. He would get home later and say to the person waiting there, "That's it I can't do it anymore."

Eddie wanted to get out and say it was okay and could he help but he wasn't the emergency, despite the old man's thousand-yard stare. The traffic would remain chaotic until they were in attendance. Jim's control of the lorry was skilful but the whole crew watched for the unexpected.

They drove under the A125 and entered a roundabout at six o clock, leaving it at four to join the on slip for the A125 Southend bound. The arterial was at a standstill, half mile ahead were blue lights of police and hopefully ambulance.

The Piaggio van had driven into the back of a tractor trailer. It was a one-sided contest. The agricultural worker had already pulled his vehicle on to the verge as instructed by the police who were keen to open a lane. He sat in his cab smoking a roll up, indifferent to the other driver's plight.

Eddie had met the two coppers plenty of times and got on well with them. Both men shared the same surname. Winston's parents came to the UK on the SS Windrush, he was known on the force as dark Greene. George's family were costermongers out of Mile End, he was known as light Greene. They both shouted an "alright."

Eddie approached the vehicle with open minded trepidation. He had seen vehicles so completely destroyed so unrecognisable that it was difficult to name the make and then there standing close by on the kerb or grass embankment would be the driver, completely unhurt. Conversely, he had witnessed seemingly little damage on a car only to find driver and passenger dead inside.

He could see the paramedic leaning over the casualty. Eddie was full of admiration for the ambulance service. People often said to him, I don't know how you do your job, well he could never contemplate their job. The only time he never liked them was when a paramedic said, "You've got to get him out quick."

So what you expect then is an immediate assessment of the situation, for us then to pull apart a crumpled wreck of metal, glass and other components all that could further injure a man, fighting for his life or a crew member, to do it as quickly as possible along with the risk of a fire igniting while you're inside the vehicle, trying to keep the person whose trapped, alive. This was Eddie's reply, always thought, never said.

The paramedic ducked back out of the vehicle as Eddie, Adam and Luke got there. "You got to get him out quick," he said, looking at Eddie.

Eddie looked at the van. The windscreen had gone, the front of the vehicle was folded over the driver, the steering wheel against his chest pinned him securely in his seat. How badly his feet were trapped was hard to tell. He was unconscious.

Eddie looked in the cab. The man was probably thirty years old though age was not always apparent in these circumstances. His washed-out tea shirt was stained across his chest and as far down as he could see. He smelled of coffee. On the passenger seat lay the McDonald's cup.

Eddie's mind raced but not as quick as Adam's. It never ceased to amaze Eddie how quick Adam could assess a situation and formulate a plan.

"Spin her round, Jim," Adam shouted.

Jim turned the rescue pump around to face the stricken van.

"Luke, give me a hand." Together, Adam and Luke took a heavy tray of tools off the RP, slid it under the front wheels of the van. They cut the A posts near the roof, put chains around the steering column and attached them to the winch at the front of the RP.

Jim operated the winch slowly while Adam, Luke and Eddie watched, making sure the front came away from the driver without doing further physical damage. Three minutes later, the man was lying on a stretcher. The paramedic looked at Eddie. Eddie waited.

"Gotta dash," he said.

"OK, see ya," said Eddie.

Dark Greene came and stood next to Eddie, looking at the wreck.

"Sometimes, the morning sun can be so low that it blinds you on this carriage way but it's a bit late in the year for that," he said.

Eddie pointed in the cab at the passenger seat. "Next to the coffee cup, see it," he said.

The copper looked in.

"It's his wallet."

It was wedged in where the seat and seat back met. "Cheers that should help, I D and all that."

"How's things, Dark?"

"Yea, great," he said, reaching in the cab for the wallet. It was thick with cards. "Credit, debit, store, a tenner." Dark Greene was thinking aloud. "Ah, driver's licence. So, born, hmm only 21. Do ya think he'll make it, Eddie?"

"Dunno," said Eddie. "Paramedic was quite concerned. Let's hope eh. Twenty-one," it was Eddie's turn to think aloud.

"Do you miss Westcliff Eddie, always thought you liked it there, apart from certain arseholes."

"I don't miss it as much as I thought I would and I didn't know the arsehole was an arsehole then."

Dark Greene smiled.

"How's the new neighbours?" asked Eddie.

"Drove me round the bend at first with all the hammering and drilling, I mean you had it perfect Eddie, couldn't understand why they had to change the entire interior but change it they did. We get on fine now after I threatened him."

"How?" asked Eddie.

"With arrest," replied Dark, "for being a pain in the fucking arse." The firefighter and police officer stood in the road, laughing. The other copper walked up, talking into his shoulder.

"They want to know if we got ID," he said to them both.

"Alright, Light," replied Eddie.

"Hallo Eddie, yea sweet, thanks."

Dark Greene waved the driving licence. "Great," said Light. "Alright to get a lane open."

"Sure," said Eddie. "See ya around, lads," he said, leaving the coppers to their day.

Back at the lorry, his crew had swept the roadway, thrown a front bumper onto the grass verge and put all their gear away. They were in the cab, waiting to go. Eddie climbed in.

"I've sent the stop message, Eddie and told them we are available," said Jim.

As they made their way to the next off slip, Eddie watched the cars overtake them in a frustrated hurry and pondered how fellow travellers never connect themselves to the one fighting for their life in the back of the ambulance. Self-preservation, he guessed.

"Did the paramedic say anything?" asked Luke from the rear of the cab, interrupting Eddie's reverie.

"Yes," said Eddie. "He said you lot were fucking brilliant."

Chapter 13

At the same time, Clarence Siddall was driving back from HQ. He had been summoned by DO Gladstone. Most senior officers would couch a meeting with a subordinate in friendly terms such as pop in for a chat, or I want to tell you something over a cuppa. Not DO Gladstone.

He told Clarence Siddall to be in his office at the time determined by him, any pretence was superfluous. He had instructions to give and he wanted to look Clarence Siddall in the eye as he delivered them because if they were not carried out, he would be looking him in the eye when he dished out the bollocking.

Clarence Siddall thought about the meeting as he drove back to Langden in his unmarked car.

"We have, as you may know, the HMI visiting us and as you may not know, they have asked to visit Langden fire station," stated the DO.

He did not know. OK, he thought.

"The date they have given us for this visit is when Red Watch are on duty." *Jesus H fucking Christ, buckets of blood, why me*, was his next thought. DO Gladstone paused.

"So forget," he continued after a brief hiatus, "any immediate plans, school visits, etc. Her Majesty's Inspectorate trumps it. It trumps everything. Make sure the station is spotless, paperwork is up to date and, and," he repeated, "correct. Most importantly, make sure that the personnel are well versed and ready for the day."

"Yes sir, of course."

"Now, I've been keeping tabs on this Watch, more importantly so has the Chief and he is not best pleased that it's this bunch of ingrates whom have been chosen to showcase his fire service. Stop fidgeting, man and listen."

Clarence Siddall had to put his hands firmly on each knee. The DO paused again before proceeding. "Red, what an appropriate colour, they wouldn't be out of place in the Kremlin. They think nothing of taking machines off the run for the slightest reason, health and safety gone mad if you ask me. They are seditious, yes, you can look at me like that but I know, I have my spies at their union meetings. Calling for work to rule and the end of acting up a rank among other things. All this to undermine the Service and would, if we acquiesced to their demands, bankrupt us."

Clarence Siddall had set the cruise control at seventy, he thought of going home for lunch and a gin and tonic but thought better of it as the memory of the DO's reddening face danced in his mind's eye.

"But," said the DO, who had now worked himself into a stew, "the thing that gets me the most, really sticks in my craw is the insubordination. Why for the life of me do they join a uniformed service with a clear rank structure only to undermine it at every opportunity? Oh, they run around training school, shouting yes sir, no sir, three bags full sir and then get posted to a station where it's fuck off, I ain't doing that. Sticks in my craw. Sticks in my fucking craw. You ADO have one thing to achieve this year. Make that visit go without a hitch."

No pressure, thought Clarence Siddall, as he pulled into the yard at Langden. This is to be my career defining moment. I could do with something slightly lower profile but get this right and big promotion, here I come.

"Ah, Sub Officer."

"It's still Temporary Station Officer."

"I've just come from HQ."

Clarence Siddall had arrived at the station at the same time as the rescue pump had returned from the road traffic collision. He saw Eddie get out of the cab and asked him to come to his office. Clarence Siddall took off his number one jacket, slipped it over a hanger and placed it on the clothes stand in the corner of the room next to a wall mounted photo of Prince Andrew.

"I've just come from HQ," he repeated, "and I have good news. We are to receive a visit from the HMI."

"What's the bad?" asked Eddie.

"Er bad, not bad, no, no, no." Clarence Siddall had decided on his plan of action. "The really good news is it's when you are on duty."

"Red Watch?"

"Yes, Red Watch. I'm sure you will do an excellent job. It's expected." He hoped that didn't sound like a request. "You have three weeks to make sure every aspect of this visit is covered and catered for."

Fuck it, thought Eddie, *I'll still be in charge.* Arthur Church was much better at these high-profile visits than him. Firstly, Arthur never worried about it and secondly, he was not averse in taking anybody to task if he thought it necessary. Arthur Church, quite spoken and full of insouciant charm, would relish the chance to calmly unpick the arguments about the standards of fire cover and station closures especially with senior managers standing mute behind him as he coolly engaged the V I P's.

"Make sure everyone has clean fire gear and personal lines and PPE and full number ones and—"

"I know, I know," said Eddie.

"Paper work, make sure it's all up to date." Clarence Siddall wouldn't be silenced. *Wow, he's worried,* thought Eddie.

"Mess this up and I'll—"

"What?" said Eddie.

He stopped himself, realising his composure was slipping. "Don't mess it up or the Chief will have your guts for garters." More like your guts for garters, Eddie reasoned.

"Now I'd like to see your new recruit, please send him in."

What the fuck, thought Eddie as he left the office. I'll tell the Watch, they will moan like hell but secretly relish the chance to have a bit of fun. Just a bit. *Why not,* he thought. A bit of fun and maybe make a point or two. He tried to be sanguine about it all. Eddie found Sam Brown in the watch room, reading and told him to go see the ADO.

In his own room, Eddie changed into his overalls. He could do with a shower but that would have to wait. *It's a game, it's all a bloody game,* he thought. If it all goes wrong, they will more than likely promote me. That's what usually happens. Having reassured himself, he brightened.

Eddie came into the kitchen and grabbed a mug of tea. Seeing Jim and Adam in conversation at the mess table, he joined them.

"Anyway, can't live wiv em, can't kill em eh," said Jim.

"What's that?" Eddie asked.

"Oh, you don't want to know. Just telling Adam about a row I had with the Misses last night."

"Oh I think I get it," Eddie said with an immediate assessment of the situation. "Well, it's just as well you can't kill em," emphasising the last part of the sentence then taking a swallow of his tea.

Jim looked up from his mug with a resigned expression, knowing Eddie hadn't finished. "I appreciate the capitalist concept of marriage is fraught with problems; however, do you really want to live in an uxoricidal society where upon realising your relationship has run its course or maybe an air of despondency has crept in and settled down that the answer is simply to kill the one who once had that treasured place in your heart."

Jim leaned on his elbow and ran a thumb nail back and forth over his forehead. Adam looked on.

"With all due respect Eddie, this is why I'm talking to Adam about last night and not you. He don't come out with pretentious fuckin words I don't understand but does come out with good ideas to resolve the matter."

Eddie pressed on. "Let me guess what went on, nice meal, few drinks, got home, one more drink before bed." Eddie knew the pattern. He paused.

"Yea that's right," said Jim, long used to Eddie's clairvoyance, "as I was telling Adam, we get in bed, I turn to say good night and you know, you can tell. I ask what the matter is and she starts on about something I said earlier! Fuck sake. I said I thought, just thought about changing the car. So we have a blazing row."

"Then what?" asked Eddie.

"I don't know, silence," he said, thinking back, "then well I fell asleep and before you say it Eddie, I know, never go to sleep on an argument. I don't just look at the pictures in the mags in the TV room."

"Well that's where I kind of disagree," said Eddie.

Adam broke his silence with a single word imbued with a cocktail of surprise, interest and sarcasm. "Really!" He said.

Eddie shot Adam a glance before continuing, "If you have been drinking, whether one or both of you, don't have the argument, it colours the row in reds and purples, colours of anger and discord. Wait until the cool blue light of morning when rationality is back in control, then discuss, don't argue. If on the other hand, you both have not imbibed, then yes resolve the matter as best you can and don't, as you say, go to sleep on the bust up."

The ensuing silence lasted ten seconds before Eddie pushed his chair back, he wanted everyone in the lecture room and needed to tannoy his wish.

"What did Adam say?" He asked as he stood up. Jim looked at Adam and took a swig from his mug.

"Yea, funny enough, he said the same roughly."

66

"There ya go," said Eddie. "Great minds, Adam, great minds," he said over his shoulder as he walked away.

"So," said Adam when Eddie had gone. "Gonna try an slip her one."

"Yea," said Jim. "Good idea."

Eddie had finished telling the Watch of the impending visit and was surprised at the matter of fact way in which they received the news. Sam walked into the lecture room, looked at Eddie and said sorry.

"That's okay. Any questions?" Eddie asked.

"Stroll in when you like," said Luke.

"The ADO wanted to see me."

"What did he want?" Luke was in a truculent mood.

"Nothing just welcomed me to the station."

"And said nothing else like, let me know what they do and say and it will be good for your career?"

"No, Luke," said Sam, irritated by Luke's interrogation. In fact that's exactly what had come to pass between them. Sam had nodded to the ADO in an attempt to show acquiescence while not openly agreeing to the suggestion. Despite Sam's short time on the Watch, it was obvious the dynamic between the Red and the station commander could be healthier.

His career had been mentioned a few times since he joined. It intrigued him. His primary goal had been fires and excitement but a rank that included a lease car and scrambled egg on the peak of one's cap might be worth consideration. Might even make his parents proud. So be a grass, he didn't think so. He didn't need to. Strange chap, the ADO. What seemed to agitate the man's spleen the most was Sam's sister, when told how well she was doing with her career. Misogynist perhaps, Sam concluded.

"Can we get the net up?" asked Perry. "You said we could play volleyball today."

"Ain't you lot the least bit interested in what I just said?" asked Eddie.

"We already knew," said Perry.

"I should have known. How?"

Perry continued, "Billy's brother at Leigh knows Leo Grant. He told him on the hush hush. Can we get the net up now?"

Eddie sighed, "Yea, OK."

As he left the lecture room, the phone at the bottom of the stairs rang. Chris Everett picked it up. "Yea, sure," and looking up the stairs at Eddie said, "It's Jane for you."

Chapter 14

Eddie drove out to Hullbridge. Hedgerow and trees were budding in various shades of green. The fields would soon be hidden from the road behind dense walls of foliage. The remainder of the day had been quite apart from the volleyball that was always loud and abusive with the recruit getting most of the stick but he had played reasonably well.

He was physically quick, his eye to hand coordination good. Verbal badinage was not his forte so he laughed at crude and corny comments that came his way and had done his best to let his game do the talking. *Normal day then,* Eddie thought. A shout, politics, sport.

He parked up and walked into the pub garden that ran down to the water's edge. It was sparsely populated in the chiaroscuro of early evening. Couples were dotted around in quiet conversation and a large family with kids that ran around noisily were being indulged by all the customers who hoped they would be gone soon.

The tide had left for other shores, leaving the Crouch low enough to make the riverbank on the other side almost accessible. A Heron stood stock still, one leg raised. A gull flew close over the Heron's head, laughing. The Heron never moved.

Jane had chosen a sunny spot and was seated at a wooden table with a bench attached either side. In front of her was a pint and half of lager. Eddie sat down opposite Jane, one leg either side of the bench. "Bit clandestine," he said.

Jane ignored the comment. "Evening Eddie, I got them in."

"Cheers," he said, taking a swig of beer, "Urgh what's this?"

"Shandy, you're driving."

"Yes, Mum."

Jane thought the remark was a perfect in for the conversation she wanted to have but decided against it.

"Seriously, why here? Have you come to tell me you're leaving Neville so we can run off together?" Jane sipped her drink and looked at Eddie. His face now had the shy embarrassment of his adolescence. He knew he had overstepped.

She could ask him why on earth she would leave such a good kind-hearted man that had given her and her daughter so much. She could say she would leave Neville at the drop of a hat, ruin lives and throw it all away to be with him, if he asked her, if he meant it. She looked out over the river Crouch, allowing a few seconds for her mind to reset.

"What and be next in the long line of women, casual dates a thousand flirtations?"

He was stung by her harsh comment.

"You were the first, Jane. My very first girlfriend."

"Yea and I won't be the last."

She is not pulling her punches tonight, he thought. "I'm just saying we go back a ways."

They both took a drink.

"I asked you out here because I want to talk to you."

"Talk to me or tear me off a strip."

"Sorry," she said.

"Couldn't we do that in the shop? I need a trim."

"No, I need to concentrate on what I'm talking about."

"Must be the only woman that can't multitask."

"I'll multitask you in a minute."

They were back on familiar ground.

"You could come round the flat."

"Oh yea and if Neville found out I'm going to your place on my own then what?"

"Neville wouldn't mind."

"Oh really! He knows our history, he ain't as dumb as he is cabbage looking and for a smart bloke, you can be pretty thick at times."

"I know. I know. I'm just fucking with you, Jane."

It was unlike Eddie to use a coarse phrase in Jane's company but after a day at work, sometimes the boundaries blurred.

She ignored the vulgarity. "I wanted to sit down with you where we would not be distracted and talk about your mum."

70

Eddie grimaced and looked away.

"Eddie, look at me."

He watched the Heron fly off, the neck retracted, head tucked in close. Was it a fish in its long beak, he couldn't tell. He turned and looked at Jane, his face now drained of any warmth.

"Don't Eddie, don't look at me like that. You have not been right since the accident."

"I'm supposed to be right, am I Jane? OK, I'll just make myself right for you and everyone else."

It was her turn to feel stung.

"Do you know how long it's been?" He never let her answer. "Five years, three years, two? No. It's been exactly 294 days. So still quite fresh in the mind. Give me till 300 and that should do it."

Wow, thought Jane. She never realised how much he was still hurting.

"I know, Eddie," she put her hand on his, "we all mourn in our own way and in our own time but Eddie, you ain't mourning."

"What do you want? I collapse on the floor, crying my eyes out in a darkened room?"

"No but it would be more natural. I've been watching you and I've been asking about you."

"Who?"

"Well, just Jim and your dad."

"What do they say?"

"Not much, it's what they don't say. Not bad, doing okay. He'll be alright. Normal male rubbish. But I see you're not OK. I remember a man that laughed easily, got on with people had an easy-going manner was," she stopped, "is respected and listened to. Always on a date, Mr cool who is now," she hesitated, "who is now Mr Cold."

They both took a drink becoming calm again with one another.

"I'm alright," he said after a while. "I was having a joke with Jim and Adam today."

"Were you really having a laugh, a big old belly laugh? Laughing your head off, were you?" Eddie frowned, thinking back.

They sat in silence. Eddie running a thumb and forefinger down the condensation formed on the outside of his glass.

"Talk to someone Ed, it doesn't matter who it is, a counsellor, your boss, one of the watch, me even but please talk to someone, you need to."

"You are the only one who calls me that."

"What?"

"Ed."

"Well, everyone knows Eddie Hart don't they, but I know you. Please Ed, for me." Eddie nodded.

"Do you want another drink?" He asked.

"No, let's get out of here before people start talking."

Chapter 15

Eddie and Jim stood in Ray's garden, admiring what they had achieved so far. The type one hard-core had been laid and covered with a sand cement mix then levelled. Both held tea in bone china mugs adorned with a floral pattern. Ray came out of his back door and placed a plate of sandwiches on the low wall next to the work in progress.

"Ham," he said.

"Thanks, Ray," said Jim. His demeanour brightened.

Eddie thought back to the other day at work when he asked Jim to give him a hand laying a patio and how his demeanour that time took on a different pallor.

"I'm a bit busy at the mo Eddie, got a lot on."

The reply hurt somewhat but Eddie knew different. "No you ain't, I heard you asking Perry if he had anything you could help with."

"Well, you know Eddie, mouths to feed."

"I'll give you your day rate Jim, plus you would do me a big favour. You know how fastidious my old man is and I'd never do it to a satisfactory standard but you, you would."

"That's the other thing, Eddie. I want to do you a favour, I don't want to take any money. Not from you or Ray."

"Fuck me, you won't be taking it from that skinflint but you do such a good job, it will get him off my back and stop him moaning about my groundwork. That Jim is easily worth a day's money to me. C'mon, do me a favour."

Ray placed the bin on the front of his old Qualcast push lawnmower. "Nice of you to help, Jim," he said.

Jim swallowed his second sandwich. "Well, what are friends for?" He said.

They worked steadily until early evening. Ray had mown the lawn and trimmed the edges with the long-handled shears. He made the boys more tea without being asked but proffered no more to eat.

"That should about do it," said Jim as he stood up, pushing a hand into his lower back. "I can leave you to sweep that mix in between the slabs, eh Eddie?"

Eddie nodded.

"I got to get home and—"

"Have your dinner," said Eddie, smiling.

"What! Nah, I'm still stuffed from those two wafer thin ham sandwiches we had five hours ago."

"What's that?" asked Ray, coming up behind them with more tea.

"Nothing," said Eddie, "we were just having a laugh."

Eddie finished up after Jim had left and stood admiring the day's work. Ray joined him. "Two slabs over, Dad."

"What shall I do with them?"

"Well, might come in handy if a slab cracks."

"Shouldn't crack if you've laid em right."

Eddie frowned. "Patio looks nice next to that low wall and the brick shed."

"Yea."

"A sun trap."

"Yes, your mum always wanted a place outside to sit. Couple of chairs, little table for her books and ashtray."

"Yea," said Eddie, "get that stink out the house eh."

"What do you mean?"

"Well, you never liked her smoking, did you?"

You don't know what I like, Ray thought, but never said. He did say, "When can I use it?"

"Give it twenty-four hours, Dad."

Eddie admired the neat lawn and the soft shapes created by the red robin and camellia. He walked up the path, not daring to step on the grass now or then. He looked back and up to what was his bedroom. On evenings like this, he would have his window open and lying in bed, he would listen to the trains passing through the countryside from Stanford le Hope to Pitsea or London.

The rhythmic noise, like a metal pulse would carry the mile or so on the cool night air. The world of his youth was a quieter place. He looked at his dad and felt that at times, his father was just passing through. Ray was looking at the two left over slabs. One red, one white.

"I'll get two pots, set them on these somewhere fitting," he said.

Chapter 16

Sam was getting a little bored; no, he thought, not bored that's not correct, maybe anxious, yes that's more like it, anxious waiting for a proper job. Like the one in the Mile End Road. So far it had been false alarms and bits of rubbish. He got excited turning out to a petrol tanker overturned and on fire with the driver trapped inside only to discover it to be a malicious call; a mickey they called it though no one seemed to know why.

How sick must you be to put a call in like that? Sam wanted to get that first significant shout. To get the first notch on his belt. What Sam didn't realise but was soon to discover was that notch came at a price. It added to one's experience and at the same time took a part of one's self.

To every action, there is an equal and opposite reaction; his father had told him years ago and more recently when he confided in him over the dinner table, the erudite mathematician replied simply, "be careful what you wish for, son."

He wanted to ask a Watch member but still felt like the outsider. He listened to them talk, sometimes at night of certain incidents they had attended. He knew these were conversations they had with no one else. He knew he would have to wait to join that conversation. What he didn't know was that it would happen this night.

The nights were drawing out, becoming lighter if not that much warmer. They had completed some standard test left over from the day shifts and Eddie said, "That was enough for tonight, except you Sam. Get your books out for an hour."

"Yes, Sub." He went reluctantly to his locker. Would he ever get away from books and studying? He was standing in front of his open locker when the bells went down.

"Both," said Chris Everett over the tannoy.

"Yes!" Said Sam and slammed the locker door shut on his fire service manuals.

Empty buildings must still be cared for, they were still very much a part of the community yet when the fence was not repaired, the graffito not removed, the window broken then society had the habit of turning its back. The tramp ignored in public and decried in living rooms. For the young however, they became a magnet.

Like the cardboard box in baby years, the derelict excited adolescent imagination. Treasure even danger awaited. This particular property was no different. A two-bedroom brick-built bungalow. The recessed main entrance was front and centre. An outer door had been added enclosing the porch. It was full of newspapers and flyers.

One pane of glass on the right of the screen was missing. Above the door, a dormer window pushed out through the tiled roof. To the left, the line of the roof was interrupted where a low hip kicked out over the integral garage. The garage door, closed, was an up and over.

It had been tagged with some indiscriminate graffito, well known maybe in the esoteric world of spray painters. Tiles were missing from the garage roof. Enough to create a column of dirty grey smoke rising with hot urgency into the evening sky.

Sam stood at the gate with Perry, they both had breathing apparatus strapped to their backs. Harryoo had run out one hose reel jet to the garage door and tried to open it.

"It's locked," he shouted.

"Get a crow bar," Eddie said, "Harry, see what you can do."

"Start up," he shouted to the BA crew. Perry and Sam pulled their face masks on, turned the cylinder valves open and secured their helmets.

Eddie quickly surveyed the scene. Billy Butler was pump operating. Ken Taylor took control of the BA board, making him initially responsible for the two BA wearers. Adam Martin and Harry Samuels would get that garage door open and Chris Everett was sending an informative message to control.

Eddie signalled that he was gonna take a look around the back. An elderly man out walking his dog watched from the pavement. The pathway to the side of the property was narrow. Eddie tried the solid wooden door at the rear of the garage. It was locked. He had hoped it would be half glazed for access and ventilation. It was cold to the touch. The once loved garden was overgrown and a wooden shed was minus its door.

Smoke was finding its freedom between the soffit and facia boards just above his head. A set of step ladders lay like a capital A on their side next to a water butt. A tile broke as he stepped on it. It was then Eddie heard the muffled cries of the BA crew from inside the garage.

Harryoo came running around to meet him. "Two kids inside, Eddie."

If it took Eddie Hart ten seconds to run to the front of the property, it took no more. Two boys lay in front of the garage. Perry had ripped his mask off and was giving mouth to mouth. Ken Taylor was pumping the kid's chest. The scene was repeated by Chris Everett and Adam Martin on the other child.

Eddie looked around him. He had to try and control the adrenaline, make it work for him, not against his thought process. He looked down, both boys wore shorts. One boy had a trainer missing. Both their legs rocked in time with the CPR.

The garage door was up and bent out of shape. Inside, the smoke had cleared. He could see shelves of paint, a wheelchair and Zimmer frame. The centre was taken up with a work bench. Beside this was a petrol mower. A crowd of say ten people had joined the old man and his dog. Their words drowned out by the roar of the appliance pump. The hose reel jet lay at his feet, water trickled out.

Another ten seconds had passed. "Harry, send a message."

Harry nodded.

"Priority persons reported, make pumps three. Request an ambulance, if they ask how many, say two and request the duty officer. Then see if you and Billy can put a screen up between us and the onlookers."

"Police?" said Harry.

"Good one," said Eddie.

Eddie knelt and shut the hose reel properly. "Perry, Chris, do you want a rest?"

Both shook their heads. Chris wretched, wiped his mouth and continued. Eddie could see burns to the boys' faces. Perry stopped and he and Ken turned their boy on his side. Bile and lung butter ran from his mouth on to the gravel. They carried on.

It was one whole minute in when Eddie Hart looked up and noticed Sam Brown standing between the lifesaving tableau and the garage door. His face mask hung on his chest, in front of him on the ground was his helmet. He wasn't moving and his face was drained of colour.

"Sam." Eddie stood, grabbed Sam by the arm and turned him away. "Sam, listen to me." Sam looked Eddie in the eyes but his expression hadn't changed. Eddie squeezed his arm. "It looks like you have put the fire out but go back in there with the hose reel and check. Give it all a nice gentle drink. If you move something, try and put it back as best you can and I know it's against BA procedure to be on your own but start your set up. You're only a few feet from me. I'll keep an eye on you. Go on."

Sam nodded and became eager to be of value. Harry and Billy had managed to tie a salvage sheet across the garden, shielding their work from the public. Eddie looked down at the boys. It was the best he could do for them for now.

Chapter 17

Luke Dunstford called over the tannoy.

"Tea in the mess."

An hour later, that's all it was, and they were back in the station. Perry and Sam were in the BA room, putting fully charged cylinders on their sets then washing and disinfecting the masks. They would then check and test them before putting the sets back on the lorry. They worked in silence, making sure this vital piece of equipment was ready to go again.

Perry finished first. He had his set slung over one shoulder and as he pulled on the door, Sam said, "You knew they were dead."

Perry stopped and nodded.

"Why did you keep going until the ambulance arrived?"

Perry, tight lipped, looked at Sam and raised his eyebrows. "It's what we do. That decision ain't ours. C'mon, the tea will be cold," he said and walked out the door.

Sam took a plain white mug of tea off the aluminium tray without checking what strength he preferred. Luke had poured without stopping. There was tea in the tray. It dripped on the floor as Sam went to the table. He sat next to Ken. Ken was reading the paper. Harryoo was in the shower.

Adam was telling Luke about the job as Perry listened, nodding in occasional agreement. "How did you get the garage door open?" asked Luke.

"We fucked about a bit," said Adam, "but once we had one corner bent out, we just fucking wrenched it up."

Harryoo walked in the room in clean overalls and tee shirt.

"I thought Harry was gonna give himself another hernia," said Adam, looking over to him.

Harry rolled his shoulders, "still got it," he said.

Eddie was with Clarence Siddall in the station commander's office. Clarence Siddall was the duty officer tonight.

"I liaised with the police," said the ADO, "it seems an old man walks his dog passed the property most evenings and only last night had seen two boys on the roof messing with the tiles. He threatened them with the police. Probably the same two back tonight," he continued, "and they got enough tiles up to drop through onto the work bench and if they had matches or found them, well whatever they were doing, I reckon the petrol in the lawn mower flashed, causing the burns to their faces. You agree?"

Eddie nodded.

"Fire took hold and they couldn't get the back door or garage door open. Created their own oubliette," said Eddie.

It was Clarence Siddall's turn to nod before replying. "You do the fire report."

"Of course."

"Do we know their ages?"

"Eleven."

"I'm also writing a report requesting a commendation for the crew. They tried so hard for them boys tonight and it weren't easy what with the burns."

"Send it to me. I'll push it up the line."

"Ok," said Eddie as he left the office and made for the mess room. Eddie sensed the sombre mood.

"I reckon we have enough day light plus the yard lights for a game of volleyball, if you lot fancy getting the net up," said Eddie as he swallowed a cup of lukewarm tea.

"Volleyball," said Harryoo, "I've just showered, guv." No one else answered.

"Ok, I'll make another brew then."

Sam got up and put his mug back on the tray. "You OK?" asked Eddie.

"Yes, yes fine."

"We will do a full debrief later but you did alright, well done."

"Thanks. I'm going to have a look at them books."

"Forget them tonight," said Eddie.

"It's okay," Sam replied, the smile on his face betrayed his true feeling. "Won't read themselves."

Eddie was about to say more when Ken caught his eye, as Sam left the mess room, Ken came over to Eddie. "Give him half hour and I'll get him to help with the supper," he said.

The Red Watch all went home the next morning at nine. After the fatal incident, they had the luxury of a quiet night. No more calls. It allowed the Watch time to talk about the incident over supper and later in the TV room. They picked it apart to the point where Luke Dunstford and John Mullins thought they had actually attended the incident instead of being back at the station crewing the ALP. Eddie always thought of these chats as cathartic training sessions, especially for young Sam as he listened to everyone's input.

They would go home to their families. Some would be asked what sort of night they had, for others the night would pass unmentioned. If the subject arose, it was talked about with a vagueness that their partners had come to expect. Sam knew he wouldn't tell his parents. Tell them how the excitement of going in a BA job turned to what.

He couldn't recall how he felt when Perry shouted through his mask and dived past him to grab the first boy and then seeing the second, what did he do? Drop the hose reel, shout for help. He couldn't remember. He remembered picking the boy up under his armpits, thinking how heavy he was before he realised his foot was somehow caught. His trainer coming off as he pulled harder.

"I felt useless," he had told Ken while helping with the supper.

"Why?" said Ken. "You were the BA crew, it was your job to go in, carry out any rescues and put the fire out. You did just that."

"But we didn't rescue them."

Ken looked at him as poured a jar of hoisin sauce over the chicken breasts.

"Save them, I mean."

"That," said Ken, standing up from the oven, "is not your fault."

So Sam would say nothing and if asked, he would be indefinite, not knowing what he would say. Just the facts perhaps, leave out any unnecessary detail and in that simple decision, he had unwittingly joined the ranks of so many fire-fighters who had known situations similar to his own. What he did know was he had the first notch on his belt and he wondered how many more were waiting to be collected.

Chapter 18

Jane walked into her living room. Nev was at the dining table, poring over an ordinance survey map. He immediately stopped his interrogation and gave his wife his full attention. How beautiful she is. He wanted his thought not to be clichéd, he wanted to own a personal phrase that was his alone when admiring his wife.

Yet his mind always froze when he sought the intimacy of such a phrase. So he watched as she passed into the open kitchen and on tiptoes, placed the tins in the cupboard then looking absent minded out the window while she over filled the kettle. Normally enough for just two cups, so her mind was elsewhere.

With the tea bags in the cups, she pushed down with both hands on the sink top, hunching her shoulders, waiting for the water to boil. Still on tiptoes, she agitated her hips left and right, creating an image of juvenile purity. He should tell her he loved her but it never seemed enough. She silenced him with her beauty and there, right there was the expression he sought.

"Busy," she said, throwing two coasters on the table before setting down the cups.

"Oi you, you've looked out the window at the cut grass and the hoed borders."

"I know just fucking with ya."

Nev frowned. That was not Jane's usual vocabulary. "You were out a while, where you been?"

"Popped over to see Ray."

"Getting like a second home," he said, regretting it the moment it left his lips.

"The man has recently lost his wife, Nev and he's struggling and his son is," She stopped.

"What?"

"I was going to say useless but to be honest, Nev that's not true. I think Eddie is struggling too."

"I know, darling but they have to come to terms with it. Themselves."

"Nev, I've known that family best part of my life, since school. I love," she stopped and looked up and past him. "I loved Eve. As far as I was concerned, she anchored that family, and the heat and passion that radiated from her nourished those two men and to be honest Nev, it nourished me too. I miss her and, what's worse, I feel like I'm being pulled into the vortex of Ray and Eddie's pain. I know I'm sounding foolish, Nev." She wiped her nose.

He reached out and covered her hand.

"Oh, it doesn't matter," she said, taking a sip. "You are right, they must help themselves." Jane looked at the map. "Where are you going this weekend?" She sniffed.

"Dengie peninsula, twelve-mile walk, coastal. Jane, if you rather I didn't, well it's not important. I could tell Fred and Nobby."

She stopped him.

"Go, you silly old fool."

That's her language, he thought and he picked up her hand and kissed it. Nev went upstairs to prepare everything he needed for his trip. Jane, at the table with only the dregs left, noticed the manicured lawn. How fastidiously alike Nev and Ed were and then how completely unalike they were, she thought and Ray also. Neat and tidy, staid and exciting. Handsome and well, lovable.

How many women customers in her shop complained about their scruffy untidy men and here she was with the three most orderly men in Christendom. She frowned as she recalled her visit to Ray earlier. The cups and saucers were brought out on a tray to the patio where she sat on a white cast iron chair softened by a thin round cushion. Ray placed the tray on the small matching table and sat down with an imperceptible sigh.

"Nice of you to pop round, sweetheart."

"Well, I had to see the patio."

"Been talking to Eddie."

"Yea, gave him a trim. They had a nasty job the other night, did he tell you?"

"No, never talks to me, sorry I'm out of biscuits at the moment."

Do you ever talk to him, she thought. "So, how are you?"

"Same ole same ole."

She looked at the patio. They sat at one end in the spring sunshine. At the other end, Ray had placed two plastic pots, filled with earth, on what she assumed were left over slabs. It created an entrance to the paved area. Clay pots would have been better, she mused before returning to the thought that nagged to be released.

"Do you ever talk to him, Ray?"

Ray too looked at the patio, the work his son had done, the aspect his wife would have loved and a profound sadness threatened to overwhelm him. The cup rattled briefly as he picked it up, vying for time before speaking.

"I was conscripted, Jane. A boy of eighteen called up by the army and packed off oversees. I was suffering with prickly heat, a sergeant that made my life hell and I was home sick. My best mate Lionel had a pen pal, oh how he loved receiving those letters."

Ray placed the cup down.

"I asked him how he got a pen pal. I can't remember his reply but he must have mentioned it in his correspondence because two weeks later, I received a letter from a girl called Eve, saying she would be happy to write to me and boy could she write, pages and pages in every fortnightly mail. I never knew why she continued because quite frankly, my replies, which are still up there in our bedroom, were pathetic."

"And Eve's letters, Ray, do you still have them?"

"No Jane, not one. I lost the lot, always thought that bastard sergeant had something to do with them but I had no proof. When I came home, we met up at the Roundhouse in Dagenham. We had a few drinks and," he looked at Jane and smiled, "well, let's say we were pleased to see one another." She smiled back. "Then before we knew it," he paused and drank more of his tea.

Jane waited, half knowing what was coming.

"Before we both knew what had happened, before we both knew what we really wanted, Eve was pregnant. So we married before he was born and when we moved out here, we added a year to our relationship."

"No one knew," said Jane.

"No one, Eddie doesn't know."

"What!"

"You are the first person I've ever told."

Jane took a few seconds.

"You should tell him, Ray. You should tell your son."

Ray lent forward, his forearms on his knees, he wrung his hands, and there was a quiet desperation in his voice. "I don't know how." Ray looked up from the patio directly into her eyes. "I never have," he said.

Jane stood up and in the kitchen as she went to place her cup alongside Nev's in the dishwasher, it fell on the floor breaking in two.

"What you done now, dopey draws?" Nev was behind her.

Jane stood up with the pieces in her hand. Her eyes brimmed.

"Oh c'mon, it's not that bad," he said. "I was joking," and taking the shards, he placed them in the sink. He held her shoulders and kissed her on the cheek before wrapping his arms around his wife and her troubled heart.

Chapter 19

Clarence Siddall was determined to ensure the visit by the HMI would go as well as possible. With this in mind, he called Eddie Hart in to his office.

"Good morning, Temporary Station Officer."

"Good morning, Assistant Divisional Officer."

"How are the preparations coming along for the visit by the HMI?"

"Fine," Eddie lied.

"Excellent, so with that in mind I want to see the Watch drill. No doubt everyone has noticed the scenario that I asked the Blue to stage before they went home so everyone has had time to think about it and what will be their best approach. Bearing in mind, they will not get the same prior warning on the big day."

"Ok," said Eddie. "I'll go and surprise them."

He stopped at the door when Clarence Siddall spoke. "One more thing, Eddie."

Hmm familiarity, thought Eddie. What now?

"The commendations you requested for your crew. They have been refused."

"Why?"

"It was considered inappropriate at this time. They will all receive letters in praise of their actions to go on their personal records."

Eddie was now at the desk, leaning on his knuckles, looking down on Clarence Siddall.

"Please explain how the actions taking by my crew at that incident are considered inappropriate," Eddie snapped.

"They died, Eddie. It's because the boys died. Commendations are made public. The top floor thought it might seem inappropriate because they weren't saved."

"There are times in this job when I have despaired but this is a new low. They could have waited a month before arranging a quiet ceremony here at the station and if they really wanted to, they would have."

They stared at each other. "Come on then."

"What?"

"You can come and tell them."

"No Eddie, you are the one for that."

For the first time in a long time, Eddie thought he saw behind Clarence Siddall's eyes something of the man he first served with.

"I'm sorry, Eddie."

"I'll have the watch in the drill yard in thirty minutes, guv," Eddie said.

The Watch except Ken who was preparing roast lamb were in a line behind the appliance bay. Luke and Billy were deep in conversation about car polish. Adam was saying to John Mullins what a bunch of wankers the top floor were. Harryoo was admiring two women talking in the public car park over the road from the station. Chris Everett explained to Sam the reason for this drill and the upcoming visit while Perry threw in the occasional comment. Jim stood, lost in thought, sweating in the morning sun.

Clarence Siddall, himself in full fire gear, walked out in front of them and stood next to Eddie Hart. "Watch, attention," said Eddie.

The line of men came to a slow attention.

"Stand at ease," said Clarence Siddall. "Good morning, men."

Sam said, "Good morning, sir."

"As you are aware Her Majesty's Inspectors have chosen Langden fire station to er, to um." He wanted to turn around and see what Harry Samuels was looking at. "To," *should have prepared better,* he thought. "To inspect." Leading fire-fighter John Mullins looked down at his boots, smiling.

"I want to ensure we give of our best and make the Chief Fire Officer proud of the Service he commands and prove to the HMI that tax payer's money is being well spent." *That's better,* he thought.

"When the command is given, you will mount the rescue pump and water tender and drive them into the yard where you will be confronted with a road traffic collision. Deal with it efficiently and safely with the tools at your disposal. You are to assume that the casualty is alive and an ambulance has been ordered but first turn out your tunic pockets. I wish to check your personal protection equipment, something the HMI may well do on the day."

The sound of Velcro tearing was akin to group body waxing at a charity event. Sam was ready first. He had the least in his inside tunic pockets.

"Very good," said the ADO.

Jim was next. He had all his personal protection kit, his pocket line, knife, snood, gloves, a bright red lipstick and a golf ball.

"What," said Clarence Siddall, pointing to the bright red lipstick and the golf ball, "are those doing in your tunic fire-fighter, Harris?"

"They are my lucky lipstick and lucky golf ball, guv," he said.

"Lucky, what are you talking about, man? Dispose of them."

"Can't do that guv, can't go to a job without my lucky lipstick and lucky golf ball, guv. Never know what might happen."

Clarence Siddall looked along the line of fire-fighters. In their hands, in addition to the regulation issue, was an array of contents similar to the rubbish found in cheap Christmas crackers. Harryoo also had a bag of wine gums.

"Do you mean to tell me you are all this superstitious?"

"It's not superstition, guv," said Adam. "It works. I lost my lucky horseshoe."

"Horseshoe!"

"It is only a little pretend one, guv. Here, look. I lost it and that's the job when I turned my ankle on that grass fire. Off for three weeks I was and when I came back, Jim lent me his lucky golf ball and would you believe it, I then found my lucky horseshoe, so you see guv."

"Yes, yes, alright fire-fighter Martin."

He turned to Eddie Hart standing behind him who had the biggest grin on his face that most of the Watch had not seen for a while. There between thumb and forefinger, he held his lucky acorn. Jesus wept, thought Clarence Siddall. "On the day, they are not to be in your tunics," he said. "Understand?"

"Could spell disaster," said John Mullins.

"Enough," said the ADO, raising his voice to indicate this conversation was over. The order get to work had not left his lips when his pager actuated.

"Stand at ease until I see what control wants," said the ADO.

"How do I get a lucky charm?" said Sam to Luke Dunstford.

"Dunno," he replied, "I think it's all bollocks meself."

"But you have a lucky wing nut, I saw it."

"Well," said Luke, "you can't be too careful."

Sam, for some inexplicable reason, liked the idea. "The philosopher Roger Scruton summed it up rather neatly," he said to Luke. "The consolation of imaginary things is not imaginary consolation." [3]

Luke fingered his talisman. "It ain't imaginary though. The charms are real."

"Yes but the concept is imaginary and powerful, don't you agree?"

Luke considered Sam's point. "Well as Plato said, no one likes a smart arse so find your own."

Clarence Siddall came out of the watch room. "They want me to proceed to make pumps eight in Harlow." He looked frustrated. "So we will have to postpone the drill," he said, looking at Eddie.

"Stand down, lads," said Eddie.

The Watch started to disrobe. Clarence Siddall made his way across the yard to his car. Harryoo watched him go.

"See ya later, guv," he shouted, popping a wine gum in his mouth.

---

[3] Saying of the philosopher Roger Scruton

Chapter 20

Eddie walked through his front door. He placed his keys on the hall table and his blue Barbour holdall underneath. He then went straight to the balcony door and opened it. From his fridge, he took out the tray of sushi and a bottle of dry Riesling. His balcony was large enough for a small table and chairs plus a lounger.

Eddie always thought the purchase of this flat in Leigh on Sea was the shrewdest move he had made. The balcony faced south west with sea glimpses. He still remembered that estate agent's phrase, and he had his own dedicated off street parking, in Leigh! He was generous with himself when pouring the wine. He wanted to sit awhile and think about the conversation he had just had with the counsellor.

At first he had been, not angry but narked with Jane and what she had said in the pub garden. After a troubled night, a five K run and thirty minutes hitting the punch bag at his local gym, he admitted to himself that Jane was, as always, right. Jane had pressed home her point by giving him a card with the details of a bereavement counsellor.

So he made an appointment. After some form filling, she had asked a few questions. How long has it been, are you coping at work or generally not at all? She was softly spoken but her questions went to the heart of the matter. He didn't know how to respond. This annoyed him, he wanted to reply in a manner that would please her. After forty-five minutes, he wanted the all clear, there is nothing wrong Eddie, give it another month or so and you will be as right as nine pence.

"Tell me about Eve, Eddie, were you alike."

"No."

He looked at the bucolic print on the wall, waiting for the next question. She remained silent.

"She had one frying pan. I have three."

90

"Was she a good cook?"

"Not really."

"What was she good at?"

Eddie felt his colour rise, the pain in his throat. He leaned forward, forearms on his knees and as he wrung his hands, it was, he knew, his father materialising within him. What would Ray say sitting here in front of this stranger? What would he say when given the chance to sing his wife's praises?

Eddie didn't know. Surely he loved her though he could not recall his father ever saying it. If it had not been for his father's demeanour since her death, Eddie may have had serious doubts.

Eddie swallowed. "May I," he said, reaching for the water. The counsellor nodded and then Eddie spoke.

"She was good at life. She was good at talking, laughing, singing, reading, smoking, writing and loving. She was good with friends and neighbours and everyone who came into her orbit. She was generous with her time and her money. She never saw colour or age. She was disinterested with her advice and she was beautiful but wouldn't be told because she knew it."

A tear rolled down his cheek. He put down the glass of water. The counsellor flicked at the box of tissues. He shook his head and rubbed his eye with a knuckle. The silence resumed. His eyes went back to the picture.

"Grief is natural Eddie, it's how you respond to it."

He left the session, knowing he hadn't been responding very well. What he didn't know, his mind in a fog, if it was the counsellor who had told him.

He finished the glass of wine then picked up a small wheel of rice wrapped in seaweed with a tiny piece of cucumber as the axle. *Why do I buy this pretentious shit?* He thought. I could murder a burger.

Chapter 21

Follow the river Thames eastward for some six miles starting at the Crooked Billet in Old Leigh, a public house where Henry the Eighth would billet his navy then past the Ray Gut, the Crowstone and around the pier and set your sights for Thorpe Bay.

Here Clarence Siddall was at home after his busy day. He had brought home a pizza and sat at the table eating while making notes about the eight-pump fire he had attended earlier. He would be back in Harlow in the coming week to debrief the incident and he wanted to commit his thoughts to paper while they were fresh in his mind.

It had gone well, he thought. Upon arrival, a Station Officer appraised him of the situation, another joining them to listen in. He gave a couple of orders that from the confident nods of approval from the two officers meant they agreed with his decisions. He admonished a fire-fighter, who was at the rear of an appliance, pump operating, for not wearing a helmet.

Clarence Siddall then hoped the situation wouldn't escalate and require something more of him. Wouldn't reveal him to be wanting of leadership and undermine any chance of promotion should something go wrong. How many times in his career had he imagined a tap on the shoulder and upon turning be greeted by the spectre of DO Gladstone with his entourage.

"ADO, it's over," he would say, "you've been found out, found wanting." It was a waking nightmare for him.

Daymare, he said to himself and wondered as he tore another triangle of spicy pepperoni from the box, if that was a word. It didn't happen today, in fact the opposite so he wanted to press home a job well done with a professional debrief. He might give Leo Grant a call, ask him how he was and then drop the incident into the conversation. Leo was a gossip that could be used to his advantage at SHQ.

He finished his notes and the rest of his meal. He contemplated a walk but didn't want to miss Coronation Street so he reclined on his sofa, the TV on low and cogitated until it was time for his favourite soap.

The upcoming visit by the HMI crowded his thoughts and pressed on his chest. Why did it have to be on the day the Red Watch were on duty? He knew they were capable, he knew they would answer the technical questions put to them and carry out the practical drill efficiently but he also knew that they talked back.

Argued, asked awkward questions and be, yes, be impertinent. It was a blessing in disguise that Arthur Church wouldn't be there. He had to admit that Arthur Church was a good man. Outside of the job, they could have been friends, maybe. He just wouldn't play the game, go with the flow, not for just one day, a few hours.

He seemed, on occasions like these to be compelled to put a point of view across that had been created, formulated by years of trade union activity. He apparently saw no conflict in his role as management and his sinister beliefs. He couldn't understand why Eddie Hart supported him as he did. Sure Eddie had the same political leanings but Eddie could divorce himself from his ideals when carrying out his job as a manager.

Station Officer Arthur Church was a member of the Labour Party and had on more than one occasion stood for election. The top floor was convinced that should he be elected to the local authority, he would prove a bigger thorn in the Chiefs side than he already was. Still he wouldn't be there on the day and if he could get the Red to acquiesce for a few hours then it would bode well for him when the Assistant Divisional Officer Clarence Siddall applied for advancement.

So from nightmare to daydream, his favourite where as the Chief Fire Officer of Essex, he stood in front of Royalty to receive the Queen's Fire Service Medal for Distinguished Service as his proud father looked on. "You proved me wrong son," he would say. "Now let's have a photo of us together outside Buck House." Would he have a witty comment for Prince Charles as the medal was pinned to his chest, probably not, and then the plaintive sound of Corrie interrupted his reverie before he got too carried away.

Change direction and this time, push against old father Thames and travel west, London bound though not that far. Slide past low-lying Canvey Island hiding behind its sea wall and then the industrial heartland of Coryton. Where the river kicks left at Lower Hope, there is a small tributary called Mucking Creek.

Imagine the author Joseph Conrad traversing this marshland from rivers edge to Stanford le Hope where he lived long before the Londoners came, a kernel of thought developing into his famous novel Heart of Darkness.

One such Londoner, ignorant of local history, was Ray Hart and he too was sitting at home this evening with his TV on in the background. It was an easy companion that spoke to him but when he shouted in anger at what his friend was saying, it never argued back, letting Ray have his way and thereby default allowing him the misconception that his views were correct.

This evening, he was ignoring his mate who was being a bit of a bore about the state of the world and the prevailing economic gloom. Ray had more important things on his mind. He was contemplating selling the house and maybe moving back to London.

To be near his club and his acquaintances would be the fillip he needed. *But I've just had the patio done,* he thought, *for Eve and what would Eddie say to selling the home he grew up in*. Naked reality told him he could do what he wanted, a sense of duty told him otherwise. Ray was unsure and confusing himself.

Eve would know. Would make it so simple. She could balance head and heart, never letting one dominate, always choosing the right one for each decision. He missed her. My God, she was so vibrant, such a force of nature. He couldn't stand her untidiness or her smoking and her cooking, well. He sat smiling with the Daily Mail in his lap, the evening sun shining upon her plastic daffs that he wasn't ready to throw out just yet.

He thought back to the day he suggested that he cook more.

"Well, if you honestly think you can cook better than I can, give it a go squire but be prepared for constructive criticism," she said, looking over her book.

He couldn't see her mouth but knew from her eyes, she was smiling. She never did criticise his dishes nor did she praise them. She was too involved at the meal table telling him about her day or reading out loud to him while she ate. How he abhorred that trait. She read poetry to him though he asked her not to.

"Okay, okay," she said, "but just listen to this," and ignoring his request made him sit and listen anyway and sure enough like the bored schoolboy seeing through the dissipating fog, he came to like her outpourings. Well, one or two.

There was a line by Larkin, it was always Larkin that touched him that had relevance. He stroked his chin. What was it?

'An only life can take.'

No, it wouldn't come. He arose and went to her bookcase. He ran his finger over the spines until he saw it. Phillip Larkin Collected Poems. Three maybe four minutes of page turning and there it was on page 208. The poem, Aubade, was he remembered one of her favourites. She read it aloud even made him read it and there it was in the second verse.

'An only life can take so long to climb.

Clear of its wrong beginnings, and may never…'[4]

He fanned the pages, looking for something. Eve's secretive time capsule maybe. It fell out and fluttered to the carpet face down. Ray stooped to pick up the scrap of paper for that's all it was and turning it over, read the message in her hand writing.

'Spuds, sausages tin of peas, tin of beans, Oxo.'

A far cry from the letters he received in the army. How wonderful it would have been to have left them to her son, he thought. So perhaps the house belonged to Eddie with all the memories it contained. He would speak to his son about it.

Ray placed the piece of paper back in the tome and put it back on the shelf from where it came. Like the vase of plastic daffodils, it wasn't time yet.

---

[4] *Aubade* by Phillip Larkin

Chapter 22

To the rear of the small industrial park lay an unused yard. The concrete was under attack from the small trees and grasses that were eager to reclaim what was rightfully theirs. A hedgerow hid a culvert where wild garlic mustard grew. Orange tip butterflies were busy laying eggs behind its flowers in the late morning sunshine.

It was a very large skip, open at one end and left behind when the factory had closed. The perimeter fence had been breached and nearby residents had been slowly filling the container. There was amongst the hard-core, chain link fence, tyres and a bike frame, a smouldering fire. On top of the detritus were countless black plastic sacks, adding to the smoky miasma emanating from within.

Sam had the hose reel and was jetting water as best he could at the heart of the problem. Luke stood behind, far enough not to get wet from the spray back. Lff John Mullins stood at the back of the pump in idle conversation with Adam who was pump operating. They watched the two younger members of their watch.

"You ain't never gonna put that out like that," said Luke. "Give me the hose reel." Sam duly obliged.

"Pull all that crap out and start to open the pile up. I'll give it a drink as you go." Sam started pulling at the rubbish, trying to get to the seat of the fire.

A jet of water hit Sam just behind his right ear. He turned. "Sorry," said Luke. "Missed."

"Very funny," said Sam, pulling at a fence post and getting nowhere.

"You are gonna have to start shifting them sacks at the top I reckon," stated Luke.

"How about lending a hand?"

"I'm covering you with the hose reel." Luke loved having someone junior to himself on the Watch. Sam looked at the wall of black plastic in front of him.

Reaching up, he grabbed a sack near the summit and pulled. Some fell past him creating a new pile. The one in Sam's gloved hands broke open, depositing household waste all over his tunic. He looked down at some ketchup on his chest before he noticed the shit filled nappy open on his shoulder like a surreal epaulette.

Sam threw the stinking nappy with such haste that it left a trail of ordure from his shoulder across the fallen bags and up the wall of the skip. He turned to Luke in utter contempt for his colleague. Luke shrugged and said, "Poo!"

He held the hose reel up. "Shall I?" He asked.

For the first time since entering the fire service, Sam felt a twinge of regret for the world of academia.

John Mullins strolled over. "You two gonna stop fucking about and put this fire out?"

Chapter 23

Meanwhile, Clarence Siddall had driven to SHQ for a chat with his mate, Leo Grant. They sat in the subsidised restaurant with mugs of thin tea. It's not just the price that's cheap, he thought. Leo had positioned himself at a table where he could watch passers-by and be ready to raise a hand in friendly salutation to a senior officer.

Clarence Siddall was irked by Leo's demeanour, he wanted his undivided attention and for once wasn't that keen to be noticed and asked about his own attendance.

"Leo, I want to talk."

"Yes, my friend, fire away. We haven't had chance for a catch up really since when, let me think since that night in Leigh when we tried pulling that couple of delightful young sorts, well I thought they were delightful until we sat down."

"Leo."

"And your line of patter, how corny was that, did you believe they were lesbians, I never."

"Leo!" It was the loudest whisper he could manage.

"Sorry, you were saying. Morning, sir."

Clarence Siddall was at the point of quiet despair when Leo Grant took a sip from his mug, looked at Clarence Siddall and focused.

"I want some advice or help, I'm not sure which, about a problem that is giving me sleepless nights." Leo leaned forward, *this sounds good,* he thought.

"Go on."

"The HMI."

"Yeahs."

"As you know, they are coming to Langden. I haven't got a problem with that. Pleased to meet them in fact. It just the day they're coming."

He looked at Leo Grant in mild reverence.

"Red Watch," said Leo.

"Any other Watch would have been plain sailing but Red Watch."

"Not that bad surely, I know they can be a contrary bunch but they know their stuff, won't let you down."

"Exactly, contrary. They argue and talk back, openly laugh. It's just one big joke to them."

"I'm sure it's not," said Leo.

Clarence Siddall had opened the floodgates.

"This morning, I had them drill for me after an earlier abortive attempt. Just a drill dummy under an old scrap car. Instead of using the correct equipment and following procedure, they lifted the car and pulled the dummy out. When I remonstrated with them, they just said," Clarence Siddall aped their voices, "he's out guv ain't he, yea guv be on his way to hospital now guv, first hour is crucial guv."

Leo Grant was finding it hard not to laugh. "They won't behave like that on the day."

"They will. I know they will. I'm just glad Arthur Church is sick."

"Why, I rather like old Arthur, pleasant. Shame his wife died. Stroke, wasn't it?"

"Yes, yes, pleasant in the disarming Arthur Church way then slowly, slyly he attacks like a snake in the grass, a so-called fact here, a reference there, full of false bonhomie with the VIPs while the Chief fumes as he is forced to remain mute as convention dictates."

"So what can I do to help you?" Leo asked.

"Is there any way the date can be changed to another Watch?"

"Only the HMI can change the date and they would smell a rat if we suggested it."

"There must be something, some way to—"

"Listen," said Leo Grant firmly.

Clarence Siddall sat back in his chair and looked out the windows at the beautiful spring day. "Get a grip. You are behaving like a man about to lose his career."

"Exactly."

"Rubbish. Eddie Hart will be in charge then, yea?"

"Yes."

"Get him in the office and give him a little pep talk. Tell him how it is important that a good show is put on for all the Service, that sort of thing. I know Eddie, he will support you and rally the troops, so to speak. I'm sure."

Clarence Siddall had stopped listening. His gaze averted to a vague horizon. *There has got to be a way,* he thought.

Leo walked him to the front door. "How about another drink sometime," he said. "I've found this bar that has an over something night could be fun. What say you?"

"Over something."

"Yes, can't remember if it was thirty or thirty-five."

"But could be fifty."

Leo looked at Clarence Siddall square on. "You need a night out," he said.

Driving back to Langden, Clarence Siddall was deep in thought. On this one day could hinge so much. Leo hadn't come up with a solution but the advice hit home, get a grip, yes he was right. The radio crackled into life. He listened to Langden's water tender being ordered to a house fire then within seconds, the rescue pump proceeding to the same incident.

He grabbed his radio handset and booked proceeding. *Right,* he thought, *let's get a grip.*

Chapter 24

The water tender was in attendance quickly. The private two storey flat block was not that far from the skip fire now extinguished. The young woman was waiting for them at the common entrance to the building.

"It's okay, it's okay, it's out," she said. "Gave me a shock so I called."

"You done the right thing," said John Mullins. "Show me where please," then turning to Luke and Sam, "take your sets off then come in."

The two young fire-fighters were placing the BA sets back in their cradles in the rear of the cab. Sam's tunic was soaking wet after being hosed down.

"You know the other night, the two kids," said Luke.

"Yes," Sam still had the hump with him.

"Well sometimes it's a shitty job and sometimes it's a shitty job, get my drift."

"Eloquence personified," said Sam. Then laughed at Luke's stupid expression.

The rescue pump and the ADO arrived at the same time. Eddie jumped down from the cab.

"What we got?" asked Clarence Siddall as he walked up to him.

"Give me a chance to get off the lorry."

They were met by John Mullins. His debrief was clear and concise. Young woman, works in the city, came home early, could smell smoke as she opened the front door. Went into her bedroom where one corner of her room about twenty-five percent had been alight. The only ignition source was her bedside lamp.

"She was lucky it never flashed over," said the ADO. "So faulty electrics?"

"No guv, I don't think so, she embarrassingly admitted to putting a scarf over the shade for ambience, so I reckon she left it on when she went to work."

Before Clarence Siddall could speak, Eddie said, "Let's make sure John," he was interrupted in turn by John.

"I am Eddie, the mattress was alight so we are gonna get it out here on the lawn and soak it."

"Good," said Eddie, and turning to Jim, "give 'em a hand."

Jim nodded and the three men walked into the building with the ADO close behind.

Lucy looked at the burnt remnants of her bedroom spread out before her on the grassed area in front of the flat block. She wore a dark brown pencil dress and matching jacket that covered a white tie neck blouse. The jacket's three-quarter length sleeves revealed a designer watch on her left arm and a simple yet not unsubstantial silver bracelet on the opposite wrist.

This completed her jewellery. The suit was a snug fit. She watched two of the fire-fighters. They had torn open her mattress and were idly playing a gentle stream of water inside it. The one stain, had it been on show would have mortified her. At least the burnt area had saved her blushes if nothing else. The fire-fighter with the hose didn't look old enough to be a fire-fighter, she thought.

His blond sweaty hair stood up over a smooth forehead and his round face and rosy cheeks reminded her of Herge's cartoon character. His mate, say five years older, was more her type, rugged. The hairline was in retreat, but the eyes, a penetrating blue were more than adequate compensation. She could just make out a small tattoo on his neck.

Luke looked up and smiled, Lucy returned it and moved a little closer. Luke joined her. "Just making sure," she said.

"Yea. You OK, always a shock when something like this happens."

"I'm fine, just so embarrassed."

"Lots of people say that. Only natural, I suppose."

"You must see plenty of embarrassing situations."

"From time to time, yea." He wiped one palm over the other. "But we are always discreet." He smiled at her.

She pushed her fingers up into the back of her hair.

"Don't worry, once you get straight again, you'll laugh about this."

"You wouldn't know of someone who could help me get straight, would you?"

There can come a time when the conversation of two interlocutors becomes mute. The eyes take over. The unblinking stare held and returned in a heartbeat conveys perfectly the weight of their silent discourse.

Luke looked down at his hands for a second time. "I never wear my wedding ring to work. Health and Safety." He threw a nod in Sam's direction. "It's him you want."

"What, Tin Tin, no thanks."

In the bedroom, Jim was cutting away the burnt carpet and inspecting the floorboards. Harryoo was in the loft space, checking if the fire had popped through anywhere. Clarence Siddall stood next to Eddie on the first-floor landing.

"Half your crew are incorrectly dressed, including yourself, I might add and no one is footing that ladder into the loft."

Eddie remained silent.

"Well."

"Harry will give a shout when he wants to come down and the fire gear is for protection, which at the moment is not required in full."

"What of Health and Safety, what would you do should one of them injure themselves?"

"Foot the ladder," shouted Harry from the loft hatch.

Eddie placed a boot on the bottom round and both hands on the strings. "We will make something up," was his sarcastic response.

Harry came down the ladder. "It's fine up there Eddie, apart from the cobwebs. Messed me hair up." He looked at Eddie then Clarence Siddall. "What," he said.

"Ken was singing along with the radio," Ken sung along to the radio. It was going to be a late lunch but the dinner of quiche and chips was plated up and in the warming cabinet. Gretchen had gone home. Chris sat at the counter with the local rag. Despite being hungry, they would both wait for the rest of the Watch to return.

"Glad I got the boy to end his attempt at veganism," said Ken as he made a list for the rest of the tour. "I can handle a normal veggie."

"Is he having the quiche?" asked Chris as he licked a finger to turn a page.

"Yea, can't wait, it's one of Gretchen's best."

"Thought the quiche had bacon in it."

"Yea but I got Gretchen to cut it up really small." The two lorries roared into the yard. "At last," said Ken.

Chapter 25

Before they got up from the mess table, Eddie wanted to say something. "Lads." They knew the tone. "About the HMI visit. Before we left the flat job, I had a conversation with the ADO. Basically, I think he's bricking it, especially after the drill this morning."

"Christ sake," said John Mullins. "What's a matter with the bloke? If we hadn't picked up that skip alight, we would have done another drill to his satisfaction." John loaded the last word of his sentence with derision.

"We know that," said Eddie, "and I think he does as well. He seems to think however, it's his," Eddie paused, searching for the right phrase.

"Karma," said Sam.

"Yea that's right, it's preordained to be a disaster."

"Nice one, Tin," said Adam. Word was getting round.

Sam raised an eyebrow but was getting used to Watch life. All would be revealed, eventually.

"Anyway," Eddie continued, "while I'm not concerned about Clarence Siddall's aspirations, I do care about our reputation. And," he held up his hand, "before you all start shouting the odds, I know you will do your best on the day but I want to reinforce this point." He paused for emphasis. "Do not give the powers that be the opportunity to jump all over us even split the Watch up."

"Can we play volleyball?" said Perry.

Eddie looked at the happy go lucky bunch around the table. His compadres, men who watched out for one another in the most dangerous of situations. Would love be too strong a word? *No,* he thought.

"Why not."

"We'll put the net up," said Adam and Perry.

"Dishes," shouted Ken.

The plates were scraped and placed in the dishwasher. Sam slid the triangle of quiche off his plate on to a saucer. Someone would have it later. He turned, alone now in the kitchen with Ken who was watching.

"How about I bring in a few things for myself and you just give me the vegetables and desserts?" said Sam.

Ken looked across at the young, intelligent man opposite. Ken knew Sam's karma was everything Clarence Siddall dreamed of and would never achieve. Ken allowed himself the hint of a smile. "Fucking recruits," he said.

As they made their way out to the yard, John Mullins asked Eddie why the ADO was still at the flat when they left. "Duty officers are usually the first away," said John.

"Well, it hadn't started well when he first arrived but he must have thought better of it and ended up offering to help me. Get the crew back for lunch, I'll get all the details from the woman."

"Oh yea."

"I just think he's trying every angle with me, with us. After the visit, life will be back to normal. Anyway whose side are you on?" said Eddie as he stepped on to the court.

"Not yours," replied John.

"Then prepare to get your arse kicked."

Chapter 26

After two games, which Eddie's side lost, he called it quits. "I've got paperwork I need to check," he said.

"See ya loser," laughed John Mullins.

Eddie gave him the finger without looking back. Clarence Siddall arrived back as Eddie crossed the yard. "Follow me," he said.

They walked together into the ADO's office. "Sit down, Eddie."

"What?"

"For once, sit down. We have a problem."

"Go on."

"Ms Holland, the woman whose flat we have just attended has accused us of stealing £1000."

Even for Eddie Hart, the enormity of that statement took a moment to sink in.

"She's lying, she's fucking lying. No one has stolen anything from that flat or any other job I've ever been on. She's lying. Tell me everything."

"First Eddie I must ask you, why the bedside cabinet was left in the bedroom."

"Well," Eddie thought back.

"Jim lifted it up so he could cut away the carpet," he said. "The draws slid open and inside were some personal effects."

"Such as?" asked the ADO.

"Personal effects that a woman keeps in her bedroom and would not want on the front lawn." Eddie watched as it sunk in.

"Ok."

"Despite the charring to the outside, the inside was fine. It was cold. I told Jim to leave it in the room and just get the bed, bedding and carpet out. Is that where she claims the money was?"

"Yes, in an envelope. Her holiday money that she had been adding to for the best part of seven months."

Eddie's mind was whirring. Could he smell a rat?

"Why didn't she say something when we were there and why on this occasion did you offer to remain and get her details and," Eddie almost shouted the conjunction, "where have you been for the last couple of hours?"

"Don't you dare think I've got something to do with this?"

"Well, tell me and what's with the Eddie all the time. Trying to be on my side for once."

"Stop. Stop right there, Temporary Station Officer, if you prefer."

"I prefer the truth, that's all."

"That's what I want too. Listen to me. Just listen. What a day," he said the thought aloud. "After this morning's drill debacle, I spoke to Leo Grant and before you say anything, I know everyone thinks he is an irritating cunt but he has been kind and helpful to me. He suggested I talk to you about the HMI, get you on side but I thought I might," Clarence Siddall hesitated, "try a more conventional approach. So I attended the flat incident."

Eddie wanted to say, get on with it but remained silent for now.

"Then I changed my mind plus what you said to me on the landing and at other points, I thought Leo was right, get you on board. That's why I offered to get all the necessary information and stayed behind. After you left, I took her details and went back upstairs with her to look the room over for the fire report and to suggest things to help her get straight.

"It was then in the bedroom, her expression changed when she looked at the cabinet. It was as if a penny had dropped. She went straight to the draw and looked inside.

"I made to follow her but she slammed it shut and stared at me with a growing anger. I asked her what the matter was and went to the draw but she stood in my way and said I could not look in. She told me what was missing. I tried talking to her."

"For two hours?" asked Eddie.

"No but for quite a while. Asked if she was mistaken, that didn't help, she told me to fuck off. Tried reassuring her that if it had been misappropriated, I'm sure it was a mistake and we would be able to rectify the situation. She was having none of it and insisted she would be calling the police. Then she asked me to leave."

"Then what?"

"I phoned Leo again."

"You told him. I don't believe it."

"Like I said he's been a help. He suggested I get back here and start interviewing the Watch. He would take it upon his self to tell the senior duty officer of whom it would take a long time to locate. He hoped as I do that we can get a result before the police turn up and word gets to the top floor."

Eddie stood, "well I'm talking to them first."

"No Eddie, not this time. I'm not having you concoct a cover up. This isn't damage to a lorry or a bang on the head. We have to do this properly."

Over the course of the discussion, the temperature in the room had been rising by degree. The column of mercury was now at maximum.

"Cover up! I don't want to cover up anything, not anymore. I want to look them in the eye when I tell them. Then I'll know and you're right," shouted Eddie, "cover ups are a big mistake, aren't they? Fancy covering up for a mate caught impersonating a police officer while off duty. Someone you want to help and who to this day has been trying to undermine you. I have often thought about the job when we pulled the young lad out of the river mud. If you could have pushed me in the quick sand that day and buried your guilt with me, you would have."

Clarence Siddall sat there in numb torment.

"I know a bit fucking dramatic, perhaps one day you will tell me what your problem is but in the meantime, I'm talking to the Watch. Then you interview them one by one with Chris Everett in here. He wasn't on the job and you both take minutes and agree them."

With that, Eddie stormed out of the office. He went straight to the tannoy. "All hands upstairs to the lecture room, now!"

Three minutes later, the Watch sat looking at Eddie. He told them. His eyes scanned the room like a poker player waiting for someone to blink first. Why, he couldn't say.

"Look it goes without saying how much I trust you lot but if someone has made a mistake, come and see me and we will get over this. I promise."

Ken walked in and surveyed the room. "What have I missed?"

"You might be the mess manager, Ken but when I say all hands, I mean all fucking hands." Ken sat down without a word. He knew when the shit had hit the fan.

"John, you go down first with Chris. All of you, just take your time and tell him what you remember, bearing in mind you will be telling the police the same thing."

"Can they search us?" asked Adam.

"I think they need a warrant to search the lockers and a body search has to be with good reason. It's her word against ours, so don't worry. I'm gonna make a few notes, maybe you all do the same." With that Eddie got up, "I'll be in my room," he said.

A pervasive silence settled over the group of men as they took in what they had just been told. Then as if on cue, they all spoke.

"Can you believe it?"

"I can't."

"Fucking bitch."

"Turn up for the books."

"Did you see any money in the draw?"

"I never looked. Did you?"

"She tried it on with me."

"Fuck me, she must be desperate."

"Should have taken her up on it. We might not be in this shit."

"I tried palming her off on Tin Tin."

"Who's Tin Tin?"

"Who'd ya think?"

Eddie sat in his room with pen and pad, making a few bullet points. There was a tap on his door and John Mullins walked in and sat on the single cot bed next to Eddie's desk. Eddie held his breath.

"Don't worry, Eddie. I'm not here to sling a bag of sand on the desk and say sorry." They looked at one another. "Can you believe it," said John, "I can't."

Eddie put down the pen. "Tell me what you're thinking, John."

"My first thought is that bastard weasel faced inbred arse licking coward is stitching us up. He is so determined that the HMI visit doesn't go wrong. Think about it, we could get suspended, they bring in a different crew or use this to split us up permanently for fuck sake, so that cunt's career isn't tarnished. Seen it all before with these grease polers."

"Hmm. I'm not so sure. I phoned Arthur. Thought he should know."

"What did he say?" asked John, leaning back against the wall.

He laughed. "The man's confidence amazes me at times. He just said you are all innocent so tell the truth and insist they prove the allegation. He said he would come over but being on the sick, Clarence Siddall would order him off the station."

"Do you think the old Bill will raid us before we go off duty?"

"They're not looking for guns John and besides anyone of us could stash an envelope around this station that the old bill wouldn't find in a month of Sundays."

"Exactly Eddie, what if someone has or two of us. One sees the envelope, shows the other, says fifty-fifty."

"Right, stop. Don't you see what you are saying? If it is a set up that will be part of the plan, divide and rule but having said that I don't think it is the plan."

"Why?"

"The relationship I have with Clarence Siddall is, I wouldn't say complex but it is fractious and we have history. We were fire-fighters together, I know him."

John nodded.

"I just felt he wasn't lying to me. So that leaves Ms Lucy Holland."

The bells went down. Everyone started towards the bay. Perry announced over the tannoy. ALP only. Eddie turned to John. "Swap with Chris please, John so he can carry on with note taking."

"What we got," said Ken.

"Southend Hospital. Fire alarms."

Eddie was returning to his room. He saw Sam going up the stairs. "Sam," he called out.

Sam stopped and looking down from the half landing, said, "Yes, Sub."

"At Training School, what did they say to you when you got your posting?"

"If memory serves it was, well done and for your sins, you're going to Red Watch Langden. Good luck, you'll need it."

Of all the things Eddie had heard so far this afternoon, in some ways that phrase hurt the most. "Just tell the truth."

"Of course, Sub."

Eddie went to the Station Officers' room and closed the door. He wanted to make another call.

"Good afternoon. A Cut Above, Mary speaking, how can I help you?" Jane had been working on Mary's attitude.

"Can I speak to Jane please?"

"Whoops, blast urgh, come here. Sorry, I dropped my pen. What did you say?"

"I would like to speak to Jane, please."

"She's with someone."

"I would really appreciate it if you could ask her to come to the phone."

Jane was busy pulling strands of hair through a perforated skull cap when Mary interrupted. "Phone Jane, you're wanted on the phone."

"Who is it, Mary?"

"Dunno."

More work still needed, thought Jane. "A bloke, sounds stressed out to me."

"I won't me a minute, madam."

"Take over for me, Mary."

Jane picked up the phone. "Hallo, Eddie."

"How did you know it's me?"

"I'm busy Ed, what do you want?"

"I want a haircut, tonight."

"You don't need one, cut it recently."

"Well, I'm not happy with it."

"Ok, I'll be here."

"Ouch," cried Jane's customer.

"Sorry about that madam, here give me that and Mary, would you dust the product shelves and," Jane turned her head away from the client, "stop doodling in the appointments book."

Chris Everett found Eddie deep in thought. It was 17:30 hours. The White Watch were arriving for duty.

"You're the last, Eddie."

Chris and Eddie entered the ADO's office. Clarence Siddall put down the phone. "The police are not coming today. They asked for two possible dates when they could interview everyone involved. Is everybody at work on both nights?"

"Yes," said Chris immediately.

"Ok, I'll phone them back and I've been summoned to HQ. The words out, OK let's get this done, Temporary Station Officer. No doubt you will have little to say which appears par for the course so we should be finished by 18:00."

Eddie thought Clarence Siddall appeared to be a man already resigned to his fate. Chis opened his pad and sat at the end of the ADO's desk.

"Upon arriving at the incident, I was greeted immediately by Assistant Divisional Officer, Clarence Siddall," commenced Temporary Station Officer, Eddie Hart.

Chapter 27

Jane adjusted the shop front blinds so as not to be seen should a passer-by peer directly in. She made herself a cup of tea and sat in the chair soon to be occupied by Eddie. Jane thought about the call to Nev. She never lied about working late and most of the time there was no need.

She just never told her husband when Eddie was the customer and she hated herself for it. For so many years, it had not been a problem. She never saw Eddie. Oh sure, she would hear of his antics from time to time. Running a salon was perfect for gossip and a couple of times a year, his name would come up.

"Yea, he's in my old man's football team. Don't like my Wayne knocking around with him. Single blokes are trouble for the married man."

"I wouldn't mind knocking around with him."

"What, wiv my Wayne?"

"Nah, you can keep him."

Jane would laugh along with them. It was natural that her relationship with Eve also drifted away. Jane had a daughter to raise and a business to run. Relationships like memories fade whether you want them to or not. Then out of the blue some five years ago, Eve walked into her shop.

"Jane! My dearest heart, I never knew this was yours. Why I am never told anything. Look at this." Eve pointed upwards. "I've got a ruddy wedding to attend, any chance you can do something with it?"

"Of course, Eve. When would you like me to do it?"

"Now! Wedding's this afternoon. Can you believe people get married at such short notice? Look at you, come here."

Jane was pulled into her embrace. The smell of nicotine and lipstick took her back to adolescence. From that meeting, their friendship bloomed once again; only Jane, now adult, felt on equal terms. Her equivalent status was aided by Eve's youthfulness. It was as if Eve hadn't aged, she couldn't believe such a dedicated smoker could have such creamy skin and thick lustrous hair.

They would meet occasionally for a drink and when that wasn't enough for them, Jane started to visit Eve at home. This brought Ray and of course, Eddie back into her life. Jane could never judge who was happier. She did know it was like finding a gem on the top of the closet that had waited patiently in the dark, almost forgotten since childhood.

Jane was rinsing her cup when she heard the front door. She returned to the front of the house and there he was sitting in her chair.

"Good evening, Eddie."

"Good evening, Jane."

It was a stupid ritual started in happier times. She could tell he had showered. His body heat had the fragrance of sandalwood and amber. They looked at one another through the medium of silvered glass.

"So you have a complaint."

"Pardon?"

"On the phone, you said you weren't happy with your hair."

He would normally have a cheeky quip for her. Jane wouldn't laugh out loud, her smile was more a suggestion. Her humour and warmth was contained in her eyes. Jane's shy nature was part of her appeal for Eddie. How she must hold court in a busy salon puzzled him. The diffident actor walking on stage.

"Do something with it. I just needed to see you," he said.

The Red Watch dispersed to their homes where, with the people who shared their lives, the day would be discussed or dissected with varying degrees of interest or apathy.

John Mullins would take home food for himself and his mother. He would go over the day in unsparing detail, his invective flowed and when he had finished, he would remove her tray, wipe her mouth and encourage her back to her easy chair where the day care assistant had left her earlier.

Chris Everett couldn't wait to get home. His partner Jamie would be back from four days in Cape Town. They would dive into bed together and only when their desire for each other had been sated, would they talk.

"It's been a good few days darling, apart from the flight back. That was hard work, this trip. Some of the escapades at the hotel were riotous but you first."

When Chis had finished, Jamie who loved Agatha Christie started to expound his theory finishing with, "maybe it was you."

"What!"

"You know, similar to the murder in the locked room. He wasn't at the fire so how did he steal the mon?"

Chris cut his lover's sentence short, smothering his mouth with his own. Ken's explanation was somewhat slower if not as considered. His Thai wife was still learning the language and despite her progress, the intricacies of Essex idioms were still beyond her.

"I reckon the sort never had the doh ray me in the first place and is trying it on saying one of us has half inched it."

Chimlin smiled and asked if she could run his bath. Ken looked at his beautiful wife and could not believe how happy he was. He hoped Chimlin thought the same. *I would steal the Crown Jewels for you,* he thought.

"Tell me you didn't." Doreen Samuels squared him up, looking Harry in the eye with the glare of an interrogator.

"No, I didn't." Harry was offended. "As if."

Doreen was thinking of the time when Harry came home with a burnt cardboard box containing a small Tiffany lamp and so she told him.

"That was from a shop. The owner said it was damaged stock and I could have it." Doreen frowned. Men!

Adams' wife had been left a comfortable sum, as she put it, by her parents. She spent her days in art classes and horse riding when Tobias and George where at school.

"Seems to me darling, the poor woman does not have a leg to stand on."

"Poor woman!"

"Well, she comes home from work, her house is on fire and she then has the ignominy of you lot rummaging through her smalls."

"We don't rummage through people's smalls." Adam was glad he failed to mention to Marianne what Jim saw when the draw slid open. "Marianne, she is accusing us of theft."

"Yes that does curtail the sympathy somewhat but how will she prove it. You all wear gloves. All of you in the room at various times and now you're home or to wherever to supposedly stash the loot with ease. Glass of wine?"

Jim's wife was not so understanding. She still rankled from their recent argument and the account of his day added another ounce of dissatisfaction.

"What are you going to do with it, another car, fantastic sound system, what?"

Maybe I should listen more to Eddie than Adam, he thought.

"I'm sorry."

Emma turned on him. "Tell me you didn't take that money, James Harris."

"No, no, no. I just wanted to say sorry."

Perry ran home. He tried to fit in a few five k runs each week. He was looking forward to the cricket this summer and had considered going to the club for a net. He was determined his batting average would improve this year but knew he would be asked for his subs for the season, which he didn't have until next pay day. He found Rachel in the garden.

"This Acer is struggling," she said. He kissed his wife and bent to stroke Abby who had sidled up to him. "The arthritis in her hind legs is getting bad, Perry."

Perry nodded, not wanting to contemplate the full meaning. "Why don't you sling it in?" Rachel said after he told her.

"Sling it in, Rach."

"Yea, it's nothing but agro, that job. Dispute after dispute, constant arguments with management and now this. It's not worth it. Your dad would take you tomorrow and look at the money. What's the saying, where there's muck. How many does he have now? I've lost count."

"I don't want to run a scrap yard, Rach."

They both looked at their lovely old Labrador, knowing it wouldn't be long. Billy Butler didn't have anyone at home to tell. He would speak to his brother tomorrow. In his flat, he made a ham and pickle sandwich and tea in a huge mug with a picture of the Mallard on one side and the Flying Scotsman on the other. He went into his spare room and squeezed past the train set to a desk cluttered with paint, glue, brushes and the sharpest scalpel knives.

"This signal box won't build itself," he said aloud to a recently painted tiny figure, in a Kepi hat and overalls. So opening the package that arrived before work this morning, he settled down for an evening of quiet contentment.

Luke sat on the settee, reading to his twin daughters. They knew the ending and all the words. "So the giant would—"

"Fall in the goo," they shouted.

How he longed for another book but his daughters would have none of it. This was their favourite. This was his world.

Alice shouted from the kitchen. "Do you want mash or I've got oven chips."

"Mash, I had chips lunch time."

"How do you eat two full meals a day?"

"Growing lad."

"I can see that."

"Daddy, Daddy again."

"How was your day?" She asked.

"I'll tell ya later. Can we read a different story?"

"No," came the cry in unison.

Luke sighed. "There once lived a giant."

That left Sam who went home, determined to say nothing. He did not want to provide grist to his mother's mill. She had maintained a quiet despair since her son had joined the fire service. Sam's elder sister had finished her degree and was now in Chambers. He recalled past conversations.

"Your sister who, and she knows I say this, is not as bright as you but through dint of hard work is now with a prestigious law firm. While you dear boy have thrown it all away to become a labourer. A public servant."

"Mother."

"Yes, a very admirable job for the working classes."

"Some Chief Fire Officers go into politics or highly specialised roles for the government, Felicity."

"Nigel!"

His father demurred, ever the mathematician he had calculated correctly that this was not an argument to pursue. Felicity couldn't help herself. In despair, she repeated. "You've thrown it all away."

So Sam went home and told his mother about a quiet day that he spent studying and was even considering a degree by distance learning. The Open University maybe. Sam watched his mother. She looked through the French windows at the verdant garden beyond. Distracted, she ran a finger through the dust on the whatnot. The cleaner is going to be in trouble, he thought.

Felicity looked across the room at her son, remembering when she held her boy child in her arms, smelling his baby skin and enjoying his tiny hand holding her little finger. The love would always be there but the closeness she longed for was ebbing away.

Jane prinked his hair. "I'll make it worse if I carry on, Ed."

She had listened while she mussed it up, running her fingers through, snipping a bit of the fringe and while pretending to contemplate her next move, left her hand more on his neck than his gowned shoulder.

"It will be alright, Ed."

"What makes you say that?"

"I just know it. You lot are good blokes. What was that phrase I learnt at school? The truth will out."

"Do you think I'm a good man, Jane?"

Eddie shocked himself with such an open question even to Jane. He had never gone into detail about his relationship with Clarence Siddall but he had to admit it was effecting his confidence. Jane stopped and placed both hands on his shoulders. She looked in the mirror.

She knew instantly that this was an important moment for Eddie. When had this secure insular man ever asked her an intimate question about himself? Her reply had to be balanced, too much one way or the other and this chance might not come again.

"I'm not going to blow smoke up your backside Ed. You have your faults like the rest of us and some are a tad infuriating but Eddie Hart, you are a good man. A very good man," she squeezed his shoulders, "and people like you, even love you."

"Thanks."

Jane breathed a sigh of relief.

"I've been doubting myself recently, Jane." *Keep going,* she thought.

"I went to the counsellor. The one you suggested."

"Oh good."

"Yea, I came away unsure but I've been thinking about it. I'll go back."

"It's good you started but take your time eh."

Then the moment passed, his demeanour changed but she had got it right.

"There is one thing bothering me about this incident though, Jane. I am with you, the blokes are as honest as the days long but—"

"But what?"

"A thousand. Just one thousand. The woman, professional job in the city well turned out and a nice flat. It is perfectly feasible, her story. Going on a summer holiday, planned for a while. Slips a spare ten, twenty in an envelope for spends. If she had said it was three or four maybe, you know enough to refurbish the room, well I'm not so sure I would buy into it. But a bag of sand."

He stopped.

"The truth will out," she reiterated.

"Anyway, I better get going."

She took the cape from him and handed him a large tissue. Eddie wiped his neck. Jane could tell she had provided a boon at the end of his day. "So people like me. That's good. I just wish I knew who."

"Stop fishing," she said. This was more like him. "Well, my dad likes you."

"Your dad!" Eddie exclaimed, "Why?"

"Cos he's a wanker."

Despite his day, Eddie was smiling when he walked through his front door. So as Red Watch settled to their night, the news spread from station to station and the one thing they knew to be self-evident. It was a time for unity.

Chapter 28

When he awoke early the next morning, Eddie immediately started on his plans for the day. Gym first. Little did it know but the punch bag was in big trouble and could expect a pounding. Then over to Dad's to see how the patio had settled. The very first job though was coffee. While it percolated, he washed a few blueberries to go on top of his Greek yoghurt.

It was too early for the sun to warm his balcony, a fleece was needed. He wiped moisture from his chair and table and frowned at some huge droppings, fresh by the look of it, on the floor from the gulls that had Leigh covered. Literally.

Eddie sat with his breakfast, listening to the town waking up. He was close enough to Broadway to hear the clanging delivery of food, beer and other essentials but not so close to be bothered by night time revelry. He took a mouthful of the creamy fermented milk and regretted not buying the Manuka honey.

The price was prohibitive. It intrigued Eddie how he spent his money. Go out for the evening and one round of drinks would be bought and the price not even considered. A jar of honey, how much! He smiled to himself. *Should tell Jane,* he thought. He knew she rarely drank. Exactly, she would say.

He recalled last night. An embarrassed feeling changed his mood slightly. Had he said too much, he had hardly said anything. Enough though to scare him. It was the same feeling he had at counselling. Like standing on the edge of a ten-meter board. The compelling urge to dive and accept the pain of a bad entry and the ridicule of onlookers weighed against the hesitancy.

Just looking, another time maybe. He knew the time was coming. He didn't know who would be there with him to witness his revelatory leap. The counsellor was the obvious choice, professional guidance for as long as it was required or Jane. He enjoyed seeing her and while having his hair cut, telling her about his working life.

Their conversations provided a general balm to general things. If he poured his heart out, it might change their relationship irrevocably. He couldn't bear that. Last night was good though. Finally, he thought of his father. If only he could speak to him. Tell him everything. Ask his advice about work. Then once the intimacy had started, talk about his mother. That he knew, above all else would be the conversation to lift this heavy stone off his chest.

Jane brought tea and biscuits back to bed. She placed Nev's cup next to him. He was asleep, flat on his back with one thin pillow. His hands were folded over his chest, his feet protruding. It looked like the undertaker had left and the family was expected next. She got in bed.

"Tea!"

"Oomph."

"And a biscuit."

Nev sat up and rubbed his eyes, scratched his beard, looked out the window then at the bedside clock. He placed one hand under the duvet and between his legs.

"Morning, luv."

"Morning, Nev." Jane didn't know where to start so she began on familiar territory. "I'm trying to imagine Robert De Niro waking up."

Nev had come round from his slumbers. He was not sure where this conversation was heading but always enjoyed his wife's witticisms over the years.

"Why, darling?"

"I just wondered if he wakes up, rubs his eyes, farts and plays with his balls."

"I never farted and I'm not playing with them. They needed adjusting. I'm not getting any younger."

"You mean once a man's balls drop, they keep on going?"

"Yes, look, can we change the subject. Thank you for the tea, is it a special occasion?" Jane prepared herself for the real reason of this morning's talk.

"Nev, I need to have a chat with you."

"What have I done?" Nev knew he was innocent of any wrongdoing but was trying to mask a rising panic.

"Nothing, you have done nothing." Jane composed herself. "Last night, when I worked late, it was Eddie, wanted his hair cut." She blurted it out.

"I know, Jane."

"What! How do you know?"

Nev took a sip. "We have been married a long time. Tell me you don't know when something is on my mind or I'm out of sorts or sad, Jane; tell me you don't know when I'm sad."

She could only nod.

"I know you, darling and I know you can't lie to save your life. About every two or three weeks, isn't it?"

"I do work late Nev, with other customers."

This wasn't going according to plan, she thought.

"I know, darling and you come home from those nights with a story they've told you or moaning about them. On the other nights however, Eddie's nights, you come home and never say a word about your evening."

He mimed a zip across his mouth.

"Nev."

"Plus Charlotte told me."

Jane's pulse quickened. Had her daughter betrayed her? Nev watched the flush of anxiety rise on his wife's neck. "When?"

"Ages ago now. In casual conversation. I know what you're thinking but to Charlotte, he is Uncle Eddie. Why wouldn't she mention that she saw him going in the shop?"

"She never said anything to me."

"Again, why would she, it's no big deal to her."

They both drank some tea. Jane got up and opened a window. She sat on top of the covers and looked at her husband. Yes, she knew his moods, all of them and she did know when he was sad but she had never seen him as sad as he looked now.

"Why did you not say something, ages ago?" She asked.

"I was afraid."

"Of what?"

"The consequences."

Her husband's misery emboldened Jane.

"Nev, I love you with all my heart. I cut his hair and nothing else. There has never been anything between us and there never will be."

"Never has been?" asked Nev.

"Nev, we were school kids, it was nothing but it introduced me to the family and that's what I loved. You know what my parents are like. I love em but let's face it, as dull as ditch water. I always thought Eve was fantastic and got to love

122

Ray too. You knew how happy I was when they came back into my life and at the same time, I knew Eddie for you would be problematic."

"How did you?"

"What have we just been saying? We know one another inside out. The evenings we sat nursing our daughter, playing with her and reminiscing our pasts. I watched you when I mentioned his name. So now or for the last five years I guess, I thought, I wrongly thought what you didn't know wouldn't hurt you and it's the biggest mistake of my married life. I'm sorry. I knew you didn't mind me going to see Eve and even taking Charlotte with me, I'm convinced it's because of Eve that Charlotte is at university. Regular contact with Eddie though that's different, isn't it?"

"There is something Jane, between you."

"Yes, Nev."

Don't waver now, she thought.

"Not that sort of something though." She got back into bed and took her husband's hand. "I think I'm a sounding board for him. In some ways like any barber. Blokes get a haircut and start talking. You ask Nobby about his barber, see what he says about it. He trusts me and yes, we have history but that, I'm sure, means that he knows I understand him."

"He never comes here."

"If you want, I'll invite him tomorrow."

"I don't want. So poor lonely old Eddie Hart needs you, my wife."

"He is hurting, Nev. Everyone assumes he has got it made, especially the blokes and they know he has lost his mother but they think it won't be long before he is back to his winning ways. I know differently. There is a deep-rooted problem and with your permission, I want to help him resolve it and when he has Nev, I will ask him to find somewhere else to get his hair cut."

Jane and Nev sat in bed, shoulder to shoulder, drinking their tea, staring at the Jack Vettriano on the opposite wall. The biscuits went untouched. Nev knew he wasn't Robert De Niro. He also knew how lucky he was to have Jane and a truly beautiful daughter. There were times he thought life was perfect. Life couldn't be perfect though.

A pearl started as a grain of sand, an irritant to the oyster that secreted a coating over it, turning the grit into one of life's treasures. Eddie Hart made him jealous and that irritated him. For now though, he would wait and see if his treasure was true to her word.

Jane's dichotomy was the relief of having told Nev and the sadness at what was to come when Eddie was okay again. She also hoped her husband believed her. Unbeknown, her subconscious had been working since last night, going through old files until it found it.

The Merchant of Venice popped into her head. Ah, that's it from school. Truth will out. It pleased her to remember the phrase and its origin. It also frightened her too.

Chapter 29

Clarence Siddall was visiting his parents. They had lived in Woodham Walter for the last fifteen years, a rural hamlet that allowed them to enjoy the countryside to the full while not being too far from Chelmsford and the relaxed lunches they enjoyed in the city centre. He had to concentrate as he neared the house, it was easy to miss along the meandering lane.

He turned into the approach shared with neighbours. The five-bed mock Tudor house remained hidden until one had driven around the bend similar to Victorian asylums then came into view, nestling in its own quarter of an acre.

He walked around the back to see his father asleep in his garden lounger. Grass grew between the stone flags of the terrace. Greek deities were strategically placed throughout the garden, for architectural effect. He recalled his mother rubbing yoghurt on the stone figures to age them prematurely.

The goddess Hebe stood on her island in the middle of the Koi pond. The water overflowing from her cup oxygenated the pond and provided the background music to his father's slumber. He stood admiring the fish, not wanting to wake his father when through the French doors came the rattling sound of a drinks trolley.

"Ah darling, always on time, such a good boy, help me over the threshold with this." He put his forefinger to his lips and motioned towards his father.

"Oh, that man would spend the day asleep if I let him. I believe he prefers somnolence to me these days. Aubrey, your son is here."

Aubrey woke with a start and was immediately in his stride.

"Ah Assistant Divisional Officer Clarence Siddall, good afternoon." Did he detect pride or sarcasm in his father's voice? He wasn't sure. Aubrey mixed a gin and tonic and ignoring the cocktail sticks, picked up a slice of lime between thumb and forefinger and dropped it in the glass.

"Join me?" He asked.

"No thanks, I'll join Mum with the fresh orange instead."

"There you are, son."

He took the glass and sat on the low wall with the wide coping stones. "The garden looks stunning."

"Oh doesn't it just," said Daphne. "My favourite time of the year." She sang what sounded like a sixties folk ballad. His mother's voice though thinner now still held a tune.

"The Seekers?"

"Simon and Garfunkel," said his father. "We saw them once when we were young. Your mother had a thing for Art."

"I'll not deny it."

"Daphne Garfunkel."

They all laughed.

"So how are you both?"

"Fine, top notch."

His mother ran a hand down her naked shin. She uncrossed her legs. "I'll get lunch," she said. The two men sat in silence, nursing their drinks.

"Pass me the cigar box son, it's on the trolley."

Aubrey looked around for somewhere to put the cellophane then pushed it into the pocket of his shorts.

"I'm only allowed them out here and no more than two a day."

"I remember the smoke-filled lounge at the lodge, talking and laughing with you friends. Do you still go?"

"Not so much now. They were more associates than friends."

"No need for associates or friends?"

"Oh, we have made a nice group of friends since moving here. We get together in The Bell."

"Nice."

He flicked the ash on the flower bed.

"Not for much longer though."

Did he hear right.

"Pardon?"

"We are selling up, downsizing."

He had never known his parents happier since their move to this house. Before the question left his lips, his father continued.

"The business. It's finished."

"How, why!"

126

"Your sister set up a deal with a much bigger company. They were going to buy us out, give her a place on the board."

"And!"

"She got greedy, wanted too much, pushed them too hard. They pulled out. Without the investment and them as competitors, it was only a matter of time."

"I don't know what to say, Dad. That company was your life."

"No son, my family is my life. I wanted to give you as much as I could and," he finished his drink, "leave as much as I could."

"How bad is it? Do you need the bungalow?"

"No, no. That's safe. That's yours, son and Clarice will be fine when it's all wound up. Did you know she's met number two?"

"No."

"A heart surgeon. Your mother said she's traded up. I've run the figures. If we downsize, our life style won't be affected at all. I know you took against me son, when I handed the reins to Clarice. What is it the mob say? Don't take it personal, its business. I thought it was the right move for the firm and for the family. As much as you hated the decision, look at you now. I claim no foresight but you have carved out an excellent career in a fine institution. No smoke-filled rooms for you, trying to destroy your adversaries. Excuse the pun."

It was his turn to drain the glass of his fresh juice. The ice hit his top lip. "Anyway, we thought a change of scenery. A sea view."

"Where, Marbella?" He tried to sound upbeat.

"God no. Live in a British enclave slowing drowning in Sangria." He pulled a face. "We thought Frinton, an apartment, inside the gates."

"An allotment."

"What?"

"Mum will miss all this." He waved a broad brushstroke over the garden.

"Look at it. Not a carrot in sight. She's no need of an allotment. It's bracing walks and bowls." He placed a hand on his son's knee and pushed it to and fro. "New adventures, lad," he said. "Now go and see if your mother is okay. She's cutting ham from the bone and you know how clumsy she is. Like a cow with a gun," he said, laughing then coughing and stubbing the cigar in the moist earth.

In the kitchen, his mother was sucking her thumb. "Just a nick," she said.

He went to the draw where she kept the plasters and wrapped one around the cut.

"Dad told you."

"Yes, mum. You okay?"

She held on to his hands. "I'm absolutely fine. Give us a kiss."

He bent down and kissed her on the lips. He put his arms about her and they held the pose. "When will it happen?"

"Soon, I think. We have had quotes. I'm amazed how much we have made on this house."

"So Clarice has a new partner."

"Yes and who knows, maybe some children now she no longer has to devote so much time to, you know. Open the potato salad, there's a good boy. What about you, darling?"

"What about me?" He knew what was coming.

"A girl friend or," she stretched the conjunction.

"Are you going to say boyfriend, mother?"

"Well, you always was mummy's boy." She scrunched her shoulder and wrinkled her nose.

"Unbelievable."

"Just want you to be happy, son."

"I am," he lied, "just a late starter." He emptied the potato salad into the ramekin. "That's what I want for you too mother, to be happy."

"I'm fine, I would live in a tent in the middle of a field to be with your father."

"Good. The garden though, you will miss the garden."

"Yes but if it is to be an apartment and that's not decided yet, I thought an allotment would be nice."

Chapter 30

Eddie crossed the yard and into the station. He decided against visiting Ray. He wasn't ready for another awkward chat with his father at the moment. He spent a more leisurely day walking and thinking. He strolled along Belton Hills and down the steps to the river. He passed the cockle sheds and bought a dressed crab for his lunch. It reminded him of the time his mother bought two unprepared crabs for their Sunday tea.

"Have you removed the dead man's fingers?" asked his father.

"Been watching pirate films again, Ray. Eddie, butter the Sunblest, there's a love."

"Have you?"

"No."

Eddie never witnessed many arguments between his parents. On this occasion, a frisson between them made him attentive.

"You do it," said Eve.

"I'm not sure if I know how to do it correctly and I'm not sure that I want to."

"Fine. Don't eat it. I thought you might like crab, I thought you might appreciate something I done for you, for once."

His mum washed the lettuce.

"There is a tin of ham on the top shelf. I sure you know how to open that or are you not sure if you want to."

To this day, he remembered how coldly those words were delivered. Eve never raised her voice. She maintained her gaze until her husband turned and walked out of the room.

The tide was in. His Polaroid sunglasses cut the glare and allowed him the pleasure of a blue sea and sky. He sat on a bench to enjoy it. Eddie thought on. Had the twelve-year-old boy that day seen through a crack in the veneer, revealing the scarring that his parents' marriage was inflicting upon them?

Growing up, he could never work out his role in the three hander, if he was part of the marriage, had a say in it or as the product of it, was a mere aside. Whispered to the audience with the back of the hand.

"Meet our son, our reason for being."

The altercation was rare enough though for him to have clear recall to this day. He got up from the bench and picked up the small bag containing his food. The gun, however, in the first act was never used in the fourth and his parents' lives assumed a rhythm of dull normalcy and the marriage, well it lasted. His effervescent mother, self effacing father in a union he was keen not to repeat.

He walked to the pier and back before lunch, then spent the afternoon thinking about work, hoping he could navigate the coming storm.

Chapter 31

Clarence Siddall stood in the foyer, waiting for him. "Don't tell me," said Eddie, getting in first. "My office ASAP? If you wouldn't mind."

"Let me get changed."

"Eddie."

It was Chris Everett this time. Eddie already had the feeling it was going to be a busy night.

"John's laid in. Something to do with his mother."

"Anyone staying behind from the Green."

Chris shook his head.

"OK, you ride the ALP and take the water tender off the run and do the roll call for me. I'll be in there." Eddie thumbed in the direction of the ADO's office.

"Ah Temporary Station Officer. This is Constable Husband and Constable Kaminski. This is Edward Hart, the officer in charge of the incident."

They sat down.

"Please call me Eddie and I was not in charge of the incident. That was the ADO here."

"Sorry," said Clarence Siddall, "slip of the tongue. I meant he is in charge, temporarily of Red Watch." The two officers looked on, unimpressed by the exchange.

"We understand you have to do checks of the fire engines first then we can start the interviews. Will it be possible for each person when interviewed not to go out if you get a fire call?" They asked in turn.

"Yes," said the ADO. "I'll talk to control and apprise them of the situation."

"Leading Fire-fighter John Mullins who attended the incident has laid in, gone sick," said Eddie.

"Will he be in tomorrow?" asked Constable Kaminski.

"Don't know."

The policemen nodded. Constable Husband made a note. Eddie continued. "Leading fire-fighter Everett was not at the incident. I would like him to sit in."

"We are only taking statements."

"Still."

"OK, where can we do it?"

"Station Officers' room is probably best. I'll show you." said Eddie.

"And then come back to my office, Temporary Station Officer."

Eddie put his gear on the rescue pump then returned. Clarence Siddall looked at Eddie. "How are you?"

"How do you think?"

"I've been here since five and before the police arrived had the pleasure of being shouted at down the phone for thirty minutes by DO Gladstone. The HMI visit is off."

Eddie continued the harangue where the DO left off.

"So you got what you fucking wanted and we are all guilty until, if ever, someone is found guilty and then what, split the Watch up."

"It's obvious what your opinion of me is but as one man," he checked himself, "as one fire-fighter to another, I had nothing to do with this and everything I have told you thus far is the truth. I swear." Eddie was in no mood for appeasement.

"How was it changed?"

"Evidently, the Chief contacted HMI and told them the truth."

"The truth?"

"What had happened, said he couldn't see how his officers under the current situation could give of their best and they agreed. They are now going to Colchester. They are going to love you lot up there."

"That's the least of our worries."

"Gladstone wanted you all suspended but Arthur must have anticipated it. He phoned headquarters and said if they try it, he will contact the union and demand strike action. The Chief told Gladstone to wind his neck in for now but if they catch someone Eddie, this Watch is toast."

Good old Arthur, thought Eddie.

"How do you know all of that?"

"Leo Grant."

"Silly question. Well, let's get started. You want to go first."

"Me?"

"Yea, you were there or have you got that changed as well?"

Chapter 32

The evening wore on. Normal duties were suspended and everyone sat around, waiting to be interviewed. They gradually gathered in the mess, drinking tea and helping Ken with the dinner.

"What we got?" asked Billy, "I'm starving."

"Why, what have you been up to?" asked Ken, giving him the potatoes.

"Oh, this and that."

Luke walked in.

"What we got tonight, Ken? I'm starving."

"Belly of pork in hoisin sauce."

Luke grabbed a potato peeler from the draw and standing next to Billy at the sink, started prepping the spuds.

Adam arrived and sat at the kitchen counter. "I'm glad that's over, what we got?"

"Fuck me."

"Belly of pork," said Billy.

"In hoisin sauce?" asked Adam.

"With spuds carrots and peas," said Ken, slightly exasperated.

"Did you see the football last night?"

"Yea that ref is a wanker. I can't stand him."

"I thought it was a penalty."

"Look at this place in the paper, not a bad price for 5 bedrooms. Need a lot of work probably."

"It don't say."

"I had a lovely bath last night and a glass of wine."

"And a massage, Ken."

"Wouldn't you like to know?"

"I'll have to tell Jim."

"Why, what's he need a new place for."

"Ain't you heard?"

"Don't."

"Yep he's got Emma up the duff again."

"Fuck sake."

"You gonna peel them spuds or stand there looking at them."

"I'll make the tea."

Perry and Jim bowled in together. They were sharing a moment.

"What was I supposed to say? I picked up the cabinet and the draw slid open, revealing a nine-inch pink dildo."

"If it's the truth," laughed Perry.

"Yea, alright."

With the dinner under way and the tea poured, they decamped around the mess table. Sam joined them. The conversations continued.

"Didn't take as long as I thought really."

"What did you think of the coppers?"

"Alright. Weren't the Gestapo."

"Good having Chris in there, bit of support."

"Did you hear Arthur phoned HQ, threatening a strike if they tried anything?"

"Yea, good old Arthur."

"Shame he weren't here."

"Why?" asked Sam.

"These sort of things don't faze Arthur."

"He has a way of keeping things in perspective."

"Leon finds this stuff difficult."

"We all do."

"Yea but Arthur, Station Officer to you, sunshine." Sam nodded.

"He is so mild mannered and yet has an inner steel and is always clear about what should be done. Know what I mean. Eddie's, how shall I put it, more, more—"

"Delphic," said Sam.

"What?"

"Oh no, Ken," Luke shouted into the kitchen. "Have you heard Leon is Delphic? What we gonna do?"

"Get him some help."

"The Benevolent Fund."

"Yea, a week at a Ben Fund centre."

Harryoo walked in.

"Ah tea, I'm gasping. They want you now, Sam."

Sam pushed his chair back and quickly put his cup on the aluminium tray. "It can wear a bit thin, guys," and with that he walked out of the mess.

Harry watched him go. "Have I missed something?"

"Yea apparently, according to Sam, Eddie is Delphic. But don't worry. It wears thin."

Harry smiled. "Cut him some slack, he's only been here five minutes and look what he has had to deal with. What's for dinner?"

"Belly of pork."

"With?"

Ken shouted from the kitchen. "Hoisin fucking sauce."

Chapter 33

The police left as did Clarence Siddall, dinner had been consumed and up till now, the bells remained silent. Eddie joined Chis in the leading fire-fighters room. "Thanks for all your help, Chris."

"My pleasure."

"I'm sure it wasn't."

Eddie sat on the bed. Chris's sleeping bag was rolled and on top of it was his pillow. Chris closed his book, realising Eddie wanted to talk. He turned his chair slightly away from the table in friendly acknowledgment.

"It was funny listening to the statements. They hardly varied. Sam's was more long winded."

"I can imagine. On his first day, I asked him why he joined. Thought he'd never shut up. What do you think of him?"

Chris smiled, "he'll go far."

"Did the coppers say anything to you?"

"No, I tried, asked if they had fingerprints, you know. They never let on."

"Clarence Siddall wouldn't let you in?"

"Nope, said he didn't need representation. I said I'm only there to make sure they don't work you over, Guvnor. He didn't laugh."

"When we were fire-fighters together, we used to laugh and joke a lot," said Eddie.

"What went wrong eh?"

Eddie ignored the comment.

"What far flung corner of the globe is Jamie visiting at the mo?" Chris sensed the quick change of conversation.

"Came home from Cape Town last night."

"Did you tell him?"

"Yea." Chris looked up to the ceiling, thinking about the conversation.

"What did he say?"

"He made light of it as he does most things in life and there is the thing. It would be the same if I had been at the job. He trusts me implicitly. It's great."

"Yep, that is great. Guess you learn to trust, especially when you work eight miles high." Eddie pondered his next question.

"What about you Chris, do you trust everyone?" Chris understood.

"I've worked with quite a few fire-fighters in my career and on the fire ground. I would say without exception that I'd trust them with my life. Outside of that, well its different."

"How so?"

"Life's multiple forces bear down on us all to varying degrees. It can make us hide things or do things out of character. How often have you heard someone say, blimey wouldn't believe it of him. You never know."

"Yea, you're right, Chris."

"One thing I do know is this bunch is the best I've worked with."

"Likewise."

Eddie wanted to say and that includes you but the sentiment got stuck. He stood up. "What you reading?"

Chris looked at the book as if he had forgotten. "The Murder Room, P D James. Jamie says I must. It's filmic, he says. Whatever that fucking means."

"Oop, here we go."

They both made their way to the watch room. Adam had already announced ALP only over the tannoy. A cheer went up from the TV room. It meant only Chris and Ken were going out the doors. Adam was standing in the doorway to the watch room, holding the tip sheet. Chris took it and was reading it when Ken arrived.

"What we got?" He asked.

Without looking up, Chris said, "make pumps ten, ALPs two."

"Fucking cunting fuck sake, out all night," said Ken as he slammed through into the bay. Chris smiled at Adam and Eddie, then followed him.

"What they got, Adam?"

"Some herberts on a factory roof. Won't be long and he will be fucking cunting back again."

"Yea and we ain't getting cover for John said Eddie, so I'll tell Perry to go on the ALP also for the rest of the night. That's six of us on the RP. Cup of tea?"

The ALP returned some forty minutes later. Their services were not required. Ken was to get his night in bed, only getting up to check the station was secure when the rescue pump went out in the early hours to relieve crews that had been fighting a barn fire. He who laughs last, laughs in bed, he chuckled, going back up the stairs two at a time.

Chapter 34

Eddie sat down next to Sam on the hay bale. They both had their tunics undone and a mug of tea. Sam's face resembled a coal miner. His skin was covered in a sooty dusting. His nostrils were black as was the corners of his mouth. It looked as if he had applied a mascara to his eyes. Eddie's seven o' clock shadow was dirty and his hair plastered wet to his head.

Sam sat pensively, waiting for Eddie to start the conversation, hoping he wasn't about to receive a dressing down for something he had or hadn't done. The barn now a ruin stood firm against the ravages of fire. The huge timbers that this old one had been constructed of were far from collapse. The fire would char the timbers to a certain depth before that same charring became a natural protection, enabling the structure's inner core to maintain its integrity.

Inside, the barn's content was destroyed by fire, smoke, and water. At the end where the blaze had started was a carbon black pile of hay. The other end of the stack had been saved when the first crews had arrived and hit it with the four jets from 70 mm hose. In reality it wasn't saved, the fire had, like a thief in the night, crawled into the base of the stack and was burning away nicely. White smoke issued from its walls like a dormant Etna.

They had stopped with the four jets for now. A million litres of water wouldn't touch such a deep-seated fire. The stack would just act like a thatched roof. It would have to be pulled apart and so they would wait for daylight and the farmer with his heavy plant. They were using a couple of hose reels now to cool the structure and protect the surrounding risks, which constituted a range of nondescript outhouses that were thankfully empty.

Jim was giving them a little drink. Adam and Billy were deep in discussion, regarding four beehives and whether the smoke from the fire was affecting them. Harryoo was asleep in the back of the cab. Behind the barn, the ground dropped away to the nearby field full of oil seed rape and further still, a line of trees silhouetted by a morning sun that was not quite free from the reluctant earth, already hot.

"Do you have plans today?" asked Eddie.

This threw Sam. It was the first time Eddie had engaged him in a conversation about anything other than work since he had joined the watch.

"Nothing in particular. Dad wants a hand to glaze part of his old greenhouse."

"Old one?"

"Yes, he has two. An aluminium one and traditional wood."

"Nice."

Then ten seconds that seemed like ten minutes passed before Eddie continued. "How old are they? Your parents."

"They are fifty-six, born not only in the same year but on the same day."

"Wow, what are the odds on that?"

"Well my father can explain it, he's a mathematician. I can stay with him through the first set of formulas but then he will say something like but that's assuming it's one over 365 when in reality it's not because and that's when I usually fade him out."

"Your mum?"

"She lectures in History. They both lecture."

"That explains it," said Eddie, taking a swig of his tea. Sam smiled.

"You close?"

"Yea but things have been a bit strained with my mum recently." He looked at Eddie, waiting for the obvious question but it never came so he carried on.

"Ever since I threw my life and academic career away, her words not mine, to become a labourer and risk my health and future to satisfy a morbid fascination at the expense of other people's woes, is unconscionable," he said, looking into his mug of tea. "Just lately I can't seem to do right for doing wrong, which is a favourite phrase of my father's."

"What a bitch," said Eddie as he watched the shocked look on Sam's face dissolve. They looked at one another, smiling. "Tell your mum that the fire service is a great job for studying. You will have plenty of time on your hands with our shift system. There is no reason why you can't get two degrees and who knows what the future holds. You could retire mid-forties say and then pursue academia."

"The thought had crossed my mind but I'm not sure," he said.

"Just tell her. You are obviously close. I can tell. She will come round. Stay close, your mum and dad are young but you never know."

Sam wasn't convinced as he lent on his knees, mimicking his boss. Eddie didn't know how demanding she could be. This was the breakthrough though that he had been waiting for. Eddie had always seemed a distant character. He wasn't cold or authoritarian, he did laugh and joke with the watch but humour died quickly behind his eyes.

The natural tendency to open up a deeper seam when one of the men had told a joke or funny story was never pursued by him as others did, riffing off one another until the joke had been picked over and left as dry as bone. Sam had asked a couple of the watch about Eddie but his questions were met with a shrug or what appeared to be ignorance. They protected him.

This morning was a shared intimacy that as yet he hadn't experienced with his boss. Eddie threw his tea dregs on the floor and was about to get up. Sam couldn't let the moment pass, had to explore the deeper seem. "Can I ask you something, Sub?"

Eddie sat down. "Depends," he said.

"On what?"

"On what you ask, of course."

Sam swallowed, "why, sometimes, do they call you Leon?"

Eddie bent down and picked up a small stick. He ran it across the earth in front of him. Sam thought, a line in the sand and immediately hoped he had not gone too far.

Eddie laughed, turning to look at Sam. "Is that it?"

"Er, yea."

"All the old bollocks and grief the watch dishes out to the new boy, all the jobs you've been on and seen in such a short space of time, all this current shit, all the things you should want to know about career progression and appraisals on your ability, which will come by the way, but the one thing foremost on your mind is my nickname."

I've blown it, thought Sam. "Leon Trotsky," said Eddie.

He knew about Trotsky and he knew Eddie was left wing but why did it bother Eddie so much, it seemed so trivial.

"Do you hate it?"

"Nope, I couldn't care less," said Eddie.

"Then why—?"

Eddie spoke over him.

"It's a game. I pretend it annoys me."

"But they are afraid to say it to your face."

"Afraid! They ain't afraid, that lot ain't afraid of anything, let alone me." Sam was nonplussed.

"It's a game they also like to play," said Eddie. "We all play it. Look Sam, I have worked with some of these blokes for years. We have done a lot, been through a lot together. We have histories, narratives. I know their wives and children. They have told me about their operations and divorces. Despite how much they bitch and argue with me or among themselves, everyone helps one another and looks out for one another. A watch is made up of individuals but at the same time is a single entity. Have you not noticed how the dynamic changes when an outsider sits at that mess table and tries to interject in the conversation. The collective cold shoulder that person gets can be embarrassing."

Sam nodded.

"Jokes become ingrained, stories told and retold. They want you to ask me in front of them why I'm called Leon, they want to feign shock when I feign anger."

"I understand," said Sam.

"I know you understand, Sam but do you get it?" Eddie didn't wait for his reply. "It's comradeship, Sam and I'm telling you this, Sam because you may not get it." Sam felt as if Eddie had punched him in the gut.

Eddie could see the effect his last comment had made.

"Sam, you are becoming a good hand. You have fitted in well and done everything that's been asked of you. At present, you are an integral part of the watch but you won't be for long, Sam because you are officer material. Senior officer material."

"No," Sam protested.

"Sam, you will do this job for a couple of years and love every minute of it but it won't be long before you will want, need another challenge, the next challenge and that will be promotion." Sam felt betrayed and angry. What does this man know about him?

"That is absolutely the last thing I want," he said. "I left university, turned my back on academia to do this. To be a fire-fighter."

"Don't take what I've said as criticism, Sam. The Service has to have senior officers and I think you might make a good one."

"But you don't like senior officers, I don't want to," he stopped. He couldn't bring himself to say the words he was thinking. I don't want to be disliked by you.

"You're wrong, I like, even admire some," said Eddie. "It's the ones who forget the narrative. The ones who sat, like you are now, covered in soot and sweat, looking out for one another even on an innocuous job like this. The ones who seem to have forgotten why we actually do the job. I won't quote the official line but it's one I believe in. The bastards that turn on us and nine times out of ten, do it to further their own career at the expense of others. They are the ones I," he paused, "despair of. Don't forget the narrative, Sam."

Eddie looked at the stack. A small flame had developed at the base. "Go and give that a drink before it climbs up the side."

Sam got up and stuck a hand out for Eddie's mug. "No, I'll take the mugs back, you get to work and Sam."

"Yes, Sub."

"Call me Eddie."

Chapter 35

The fine weather held, supporting the optimists' view that it was going to be a long hot summer. The contrarians argued it was too much too soon. The daffodils were content with the moisture in the soil and nodded their approval. The barn fire was reported in the local paper more as an afterthought to an amusing story of five ducklings that had fallen in a storm drain.

They were found swimming in the murky waters at the bottom of the drain while their perplexed mother paced the pavement, listening to their plaintive quacks. All were rescued safely to the delight of their mother and the local editor who loved a good news story for her ailing readership when more serious issues had dried or gone to ground.

If she had got wind of the possible theft of a thousand pounds by Langden's finest, it would be front page and inside pages two and three. It would run over the coming days until the revelatory denouement. It would be worthy of comment in her leader column. Can the fire service be trusted in our homes?

What was the Chief Fire Officer doing about it? Were the police bringing prosecutions and the victim a young woman living alone who put her trust in these so-called public servants, what of her? How was she bearing up, her home destroyed, her money stolen. This account however was not to see the light of day.

Lucy Holland was reluctant to say anything. She played it down, told the reporter that the damage was minimal and would not allow photos. So it was chronicled in one column on the day and was soon forgotten. This pleased Lucy Holland. She knew only too well the scrutiny a story like hers would bring. National news maybe and when they got hold of something like this, they delved.

Lucy was still on probation with her company. The job she absolutely loved could be jeopardised if her conviction for shoplifting came to light. Her non-disclosure would be enough to ensure an early termination to her contract. So, a public response from the fire service was not required. It could remain Mum and the people of Langden went about their lives, unaware of the scandal.

Chapter 36

Lff John Mullins returned to work on the second night. He had spent six hours the previous evening in A and E with his mother, following a fall.

"The old bill are coming back tonight to interview you, John," said Eddie, "you okay with that?"

"Why wouldn't I be?" Came his terse reply.

"Sorry John, it came across differently than meant. How's Mum?"

"Not getting any younger."

After the interview the police, as taciturn as ever, took their leave and left the Red to themselves. They put out three cars in quick succession and attended a bungalow with water pouring out the back door. The neighbour was waiting for them.

"They are on holiday," he said, "and it's done up like a drum."

"When they back?"

"Ten days."

"Your place, is it the same design?"

"Yea, built together."

"Has it got a loft hatch?"

"Yep."

They got on to the roof and lifted enough tiles to get in. The felt beneath the tiles was cut out. Sam and Luke dropped inside the loft. They took torches and a single extension of the triple extension ladder with them. The next time they were seen was unlocking the back door.

"It's pissing out under the sink," Luke said.

They located the stop cock and with a squeegee the neighbour had, pushed out the remaining water covering the tiled floor. Sam and Luke locked the back door and the next time they were seen, they were coming out the opening in the roof tiles. Once out, the roof tiles were replaced and the ladder stowed back on the fire engine.

Eddie smiled at the neighbour. "Don't know about the wooden flooring in the other rooms, they might get away with it."

"No doubt you will tell them what happened when they get back and if I was you, I'd charge them for a new pair," he said, looking down at the man's ruined slippers.

The man, in his late fifties, was half the size of Eddie. He stared at his sodden footwear, momentarily lost for words; instead, he put out his hand, which Eddie shook.

"Thank you," the man said.

"That's okay," said Eddie, "good night."

Luke called out, "Eddie, got a shout."

"What is it?"

"Wheelie bins, back of Tesco's."

Good, thought Eddie, *we need a busy night.*

Chapter 37

The early morning gym session hadn't helped. For fifteen unrelenting minutes, he hit the heavy bag and it laughed at him, is that all ya got, Eddie. So he ran, rowed, had a sauna and almost threw himself in the icy plunge pool. The stress he felt would not be assuaged. The pressure on him at work on top of his personal live was doing damage. Something had to give. He knew what had to be done and today, he was going to try. He was going to talk to his father.

He drove from Leigh to Stanford on auto pilot. It was a journey he would never have been able to recall, so concentrated were his thoughts. He would start by saying sorry. Sorry for what happened to Mum. He felt his father held him responsible. He needed to know if his father shared his opinion of the crash.

It would be an unaggressive opening and he could gauge his father's response before proceeding. No, perhaps that should come later. Maybe he should just ask why. Why had they never been close, what is your opinion, Dad or have I got it wrong, tell me, Dad. You have told me so little. Mum would tell me you loved me.

"You know he loves you, son." He could hear her words clearly. You have always been opaque, dad. *Fuck sake,* Eddie thought. *You don't tell your father he's opaque, you tell him he's a good father, that you had a good childhood; that you love him. It's just we don't talk, Dad and we need to, I need to.*

The lay-by outside the house had one free space. He reverse parked, got out and walked to the house. If a passer-by had said good morning, he could not have answered. His mouth so dry, his tongue mute. The back door was locked. Shit, he's gone out, that's all I need.

"Son."

Eddie turned to see his father closing the gate he had left open. He had milk and a loaf. "Born in a barn. You got a key, ain'tcha?"

"Yea, I—"

"Well, come on then."

In the kitchen, their movements were closely choreographed as they made tea and toast. Neither spoke until, "Shall we have it on the patio?"

"No, I prefer my chair."

Eddie sat on the settee. The hot tea slaked the desert in his mouth. His father chewed the thin white bread, lightly toasted with scrapings of margarine and marmalade. He held the plate high on his chest, carefully to catch any escaping crumbs.

"I've been wanting to talk," he swallowed, "to talk to you."

Eddie wanted to put the cup down, but without a coaster, he hesitated. The cup hovered over the glass coffee table.

"Just put it down."

Eddie took a last mouthful then placed it.

"I wanted to say thank you for the patio and all the other help recently."

"What help?"

"You have come round here regularly since your mother died, to you know, to check up on me and although there was no need, I appreciate it. Thank you."

As surprised as Eddie was, the sentiment and tone seemed more appropriate for a home help than a son. Ray leaned forward, placed the small plate on the coffee table, picked up his tea and drank. He placed the cup on the plate then sat back in his chair and stared out the front window.

"I have been thinking of selling up and I want your opinion."

The synapses in Eddie's brain went into over drive. In whatever percentage of that first second of response, a myriad of questions and thoughts were sparked into life. From home help to estate agent, a thought; why, the obvious question.

"What?"

His mind needed another second to choose one.

"I have been considering selling the house and moving back up the smoke, maybe." Eddie's emotional responses got in line, banality was first in the queue.

"What about the patio?"

"I needed to do that. Like flowers at a road side."

He picked a crumb from his trousers and placed it on the plate.

"A loved one dies and we have to pay homage in ways that are pointless to the deceased but we do it anyway. It assuages a need. I had promised your mum that patio for a while. It helped me close a certain time. Mourning."

Eddie knew his father had been thinking deeply about this conversation. He couldn't recall such loquaciousness from his father, ever.

"It's nice you want to talk, Dad and ask my opinion, I appreciate that but it's a crying shame that it's taken the death of my mother for you to do it."

Ray ignored the remark.

"Well what do you think, any objections?"

Eddie followed his father's gaze to the bright sunlit window. "I'm struggling, Dad."

"Take your time then, there's no rush."

"Not with the house, Dad. It's been tough at work. I've been in charge lately, something I'm not good at. I'm in a constant battle with the station commander, we lost a couple of kids in a fire recently, now someone has accused the Watch of stealing a thousand pounds and while I don't believe it, I can't stop thinking that it might be one of the Watch and if it's true, then the terrible implications that will have. Then there's Jane. I feel—"

"Humph," Ray snorted out the sound. It stopped Eddie in his tracks.

"Humph," Eddie repeated the sound. "What's that supposed to mean?"

His fear and apprehension turned to anger at his father's cold disregard and he was about to let him have it but Ray was quicker off the remark.

"Do you think you are the only one with problems? We all have them and we deal with them. Some better than others granted, but deal with them we do." Ray looked straight at his son for the first time this morning. "Man up, son."

"Man up eh, they are your words of wisdom, from a father to his only son. Words of wisdom I have been waiting for all my life. Why I don't know, you have been more a shadow than a father, a presence. When did we do anything together, let alone talk? Other kids would tell me that they were in trouble with their old man and they were scared or worried. I used to think I'm lucky because I'm never in trouble with mine but do you know what, Dad that would have been something at least. It would have been interaction."

It was Ray's turn to get angry.

"You," he shouted, "had everything you needed, a beautiful mother, a home, a full belly, clothes on your back."

"Crap shoes." Eddie knew how pathetic the comment was but didn't care.

"Crap shoes." Rays laugh was heavy with disdain. "Is that it, crap shoes? There are millions of people out there right now," he said, pointing at the window, "walking the streets, living their lives that would have given their high teeth for your upbringing."

Eddie's emotions were flipping from anger to despair. His father's sentiment was hard for him to deal with. They held each other's stare.

"What did I do Dad, tell me. What did I do wrong?" Ray averted his gaze.

"You were born."

The gun went off. How many times, he wasn't sure. The pain in his chest, the explosion in his head, at least two. He stood up. Ray pushed himself back in his chair as if fearing a blow. Eddie walked to the front window. He looked down at the vase of plastic daffodils. The net curtains smelled fresh. The burden he was carrying had just been added to. It weighed on his heart. He started to talk.

"I came here today to ask if you blamed me for Mum's death."

"I have."

"Shut up." Eddie reinforced the command with a raised hand. He did not turn to look at his father. "I have had a feeling since the accident that you blamed me in some part because I was there because I attended the incident and that maybe, just maybe you thought I could have done more to save her."

"No."

"Well, I could have. I could have done more. When I got off the lorry and recognised the VW, all my training deserted me. The ambulance crew had already removed Ursula but Mum was trapped, she would have to be cut out. I climbed in the driver's side and put my arms about her. I said Mum.

"She was barely conscious, pale and beyond pain. I could smell her blood. She became lucid for a moment and she said, 'I knew you would save me son, boy am I going to be in trouble when your dad finds out how much I spent today'."

Ray twisted in his chair, as though a knife had been inserted between his ribs.

"I tried to get as close as possible so her head could rest on my shoulder and all the time, there were words in the background that weren't making sense, then a hand on my arm and the words filtered through, 'c'mon Eddie, come on mate, let's get you out, then we can get Mum out,' but I couldn't. I couldn't leave her.

"I don't know if she said anything else, the sound of machinery filled the cab. A paramedic got a line in her arm. It was Jim, his gentle strength that got me out of the cab and back to the lorry. A female police officer was talking to me. That's all I remember."

Eddie turned to look again at his father.

"I don't know how long I sat with her, with Mum but I do know I hindered the rescue effort and maybe intervention a few minutes earlier would have made a difference."

Ray held the fingers of one hand in the other and twisted them back and forth. He pushed out his bottom lip. Eddie continued.

"No one spoke to me about it afterwards. They didn't include me in the debrief for emotional reasons, they said. They offered me counselling. They gave me compassionate leave. The Watch offered their condolences but no one spoke to me about it. I wondered what they said behind my back, if word had got back to you. I wanted to talk to you about it but I couldn't because we don't, do we? That's why I came today to talk about Mum, the accident, everything. To seek, to seek—"

"Sit down, son."

Eddie's anger rose again.

"What for? I think enough has been said. You don't say much but you got killer lines. Sell the house and fuck off with the money. I don't care what you do or what you think of me."

Ray got up quickly and went to his son. He was smaller than Eddie but had to impose himself as best he could.

"You've had your turn, now it's mine. First, I want you to sit down. I'm going to make another cup of tea. Please son, sit down, this is an important day for both of us."

For a moment, Eddie was back with the police officer. The same numb feeling accompanied by a vacant stare. He sat down slowly, feeling the seat with both hands, unsure of what he was doing. *You were born,* he thought. Ray came back in the room with two fresh cups.

"There," he said.

Ray sat down on the edge of his chair and leaned forward with his arms resting on his knees. He rocked slightly.

"I guess I never said much because there is so much to tell, I never knew where to start."

"Try starting with, you were born."

"Your mum told you how we met. What she never said was you were conceived out of wedlock. We moved out here and added a year to our marriage, of course the London lot knew but out here, no one."

"Is that it? Is that the big deal?"

Eddie's mind bordered on incredulity. "You wanted me to talk, now listen. I came out of the army and I couldn't wait to meet this girl that wrote such wonderful letters to me."

"Do you still have them?"

"Are you going to listen? We met up, Roundhouse Dagenham. We had a laugh, we got on alright. We met quite a few times over a couple months. We, we made love. You know though, right. We both knew this wasn't the real thing. Then, 'I'm pregnant, Ray,' and before you say anything, I'm keeping him."

"Him," I said.

"Yes, I know it's a boy and he shall be called Edward, if you have no objections."

"I couldn't care less about a name. It was my family I cared about. I was petrified of telling my father. The explosion. It was the same year he died. I wished I had waited. It never came, the explosion. He was digging his allotment. He stopped, looked at me. 'You've made your bed, now lie in it.' Then he carried on digging. So I done the right thing and shortly after, we got the opportunity of this place from East Ham council. I made your mother an honest woman. What a ridiculous phrase. I don't think your mother cared. She was ahead of her time. I wasn't and I've regretted it ever since. Your birth was the product of my mistake. That's what I meant earlier." Ray drank some tea. Eddie couldn't. He felt paralysed.

"We tried to make it work in the early years. Eve, always positive, spoke of different love. She would tell me all the different words for love the Greeks have. There's a word for the love of family, Store something."

"Storge."

"Yea, that's it. Eros is the only one I can remember. 'We would love our family,' she said. I tried but try as I may, I just regretted it. I thought, well, raise the boy and then see. By the time you left for the sea, the mould had set. We had cemented our lives together and apart."

They were silent while Ray collected his thoughts. "I thought your mum might be lesbian."

Ray watched his son's reaction.

"I know you think I'm crazy but we stopped making love."

"I don't need to know."

"Yea, I think you do. You might have some input. We stopped very early in the marriage. Apart from our dalliance, I never heard in all the years, her mention another man. I was never suspicious of another man. She had her friends, all girlfriends, they had their weekends away."

"I knew them women, they were all married."

"So what. Did you ever have any knowledge of an affair? Tell me if you did." Eddie shook his head. "Doesn't matter now."

"Duty. I done my duty. Army, wife, son. Did I do it well? One out of three, perhaps. I felt the Storge son, I did but the truth is I'm not a natural father. Some of us are born to kings, some to beggars. We have little choice in the matter. You got me and I was, am a poor father. You dipped out. I do know that as a son, you have been the best anyone could wish for and no, I do not place any blame on you regarding her death. If someone had said something to me, they would have got a flea in their ear. I mourned her passing. All said and done, she was a fantastic woman and if I had been as strong as her all those years ago and stood up to my father and society, then all our lives would have been different, perhaps better. Drink your tea, it's getting cold."

"I can't."

Eddie washed at his face with both hands then scratched his scalp. "Sell it."

"Think about it, a few days."

"No, sell it. This place deserves better."

"Do you want anything?" Ray gestured with one hand.

What he wanted had gone. Eve had left the building. He watched as his father removed the crockery. In the kitchen, he could hear water filling a bowl. What did he want? He needed time. He got up. Some books definitely. He went upstairs. *How many more times,* he thought. He went in her bedroom. The double room at the front of the house.

Ray had moved into his old room years ago. He opened the fitted wardrobes and breathed in. It was her and not her. The nicotine had soured the cloth. He tried to remember the smell of her skin. It saddened him that his sensual memory was fading. On the vanity unit was the Japanese music box he had brought home for her. He lifted the lid and listened as Sakura Sakura unwound.

Was it last wound by her? The costume jewellery was for his father to bestow. He noticed the small china collie dog that he had bought his mother when holidaying in Great Yarmouth. The year it rained every day. They couldn't return to the bed and breakfast during the day so spent the wet hours traipsing from shop to shop. She thanked him effusively before dropping it in her bag.

He wasn't sure at the time how much his present was liked but from the day they returned home so many years ago, until now it has sat on her bedside table. He looked around at the decor, the covers, a photo of both of them on Southend seafront. Taken by a snapper trying to earn a few bucks. Was it a boudoir dedicated to Sappho? He couldn't tell and what did it matter. Nothing seemed to matter anymore.

Downstairs again, his father stood at the bookcase. "You'll want the books."

"Yes, please. Well the Larkin and Brideshead, definitely." Ray scanned the shelves.

"Here, take them now."

Eddie looked at the two dog eared tomes.

"I remember her reading Brideshead to me in bed. I hated it. She insisted though." Ray nodded his understanding.

"She loved the sublime phrases. That's what she called them and would repeat them over and over, almost forgetting the story. A blow upon a bruise [5]is one, I recall."

He looked at his father.

"That's what this morning's been like."

With both books in one hand, he gave a little wave.

"Thanks. Give me some time to think of anything else."

"Oh, the little collie on her bedside."

"Anyway, I'm going."

"Don't. Let's do something."

"You're a lifetime too late for that one."

"Let's go and visit Mum."

---

[5] *Brideshead Revisited* by E. Waugh

Chapter 38

Sam Brown was atop the large step ladder, creosoting the wooden frame of the greenhouse roof. His father knelt on the grass, applying the preservative at the base.

"Son, I would appreciate you not flicking creosote over my balding pate. Apart from the possible carcinogens, I don't want to end up looking like a nabob."

His son never answered.

"We are thinking of Glyndebourne this summer. Haven't been for what, four years now. I wondered if you fancied coming."

Sam descended, he placed his brush in an old paint tin and removed his rubber debris gloves. "That's the roof done."

"We could ask Penelope next door. You two have always hit it off."

"Ask her to what?"

"Glyndebourne. What say you eh, bit of Mozart, picnic on the lawn."

"Oh, I'll think about it."

Nigel Brown got up with a sigh and stretched. It had been obvious all morning to him that his son was perturbed.

"Before we put the ladder away son, tell me, are you alright?"

"Yes Dad, I'm perfectly happy."

"Well, of late your happiness appears to go hand in glove with melancholy. It concerns me." Nigel glanced furtively about himself, checking they were alone. "You can always talk to me, you know that."

Sam put an arm through the ladder and rested on the rounds. He rubbed his chin. "Work's been problematic."

"I suspected so."

"Why?"

"Your enthusiasm has waned recently."

"It's not that Dad, it's—"

He looked at a brown run on the newly installed float glass. "I don't think I fit in very well."

"Hmmm, I should imagine it is a very different environment to any you have experienced before."

"Yes, it can be what, rough and ready, the discourse somewhat pejorative and the humour, to be honest at times quite banal."

"Do you like the people you work with?"

"Yes, there's the rub despite what I've just said, I think they are great. All of them. A really fine group of men. I just don't feel like I fit in and I don't want to let them down and I feel that I may have."

"I'm sure you haven't, son. You are still learning your profession." Nigel picked up the tins, rags and brushes. "Let's get all this put away and then some lunch."

They walked together up the long garden. A pied wagtail flew low over the expansive lawn. It dropped to the grass busily looking about, its tail bobbing up and down.

"One of my favourites," said Nigel. "I remember when I first started lecturing. Useless, I could do the maths on the board in front of the gathered throng but explaining theory was as perplexing for me as it must have been for the poor student. I would look at their blank faces and believe I was doing them a disservice."

Nigel transferred the tins to one hand and placed his free one on his son's shoulder. "I know things haven't been easy with your mother since Queen Mary's but you have done well. I think you have made a good choice. I can see you succeeding."

"Thanks, Dad."

His son listened as he always did to him but he could tell from the wan smile that he wasn't convinced. Nigel squeezed his son's shoulder in reassurance. He turned the piece of wood holding the shed door closed to the vertical.

"Your sis is here for lunch. I'm going to tell her I've got her a ticket for Glyndebourne."

"Why? She hates classical music."

"I like watching your mother bristle when she hears her daughter telling me where to shove it."

The two men manoeuvred the steps into the shed together as the pied wagtail decided there was nothing of interest and flew off.

Chapter 39

Narrow lanes between Broadway West and Rectory Grove harbour, small art galleries, shops selling curios and a bar called Estuary English. During busy weekday mornings, it was home to mothers and their babies. The women nursed tall skinny lattes and mint teas, idly presenting titbits to their offspring who derived more pleasure from dropping their food on the floor than consuming it.

After six o clock, children were discouraged and the bar morphed into its original purpose. The owner of Estuary English never intended or indeed designated Friday night to be an over thirties night. That decision was made by the local clientele who felt they needed a place of their own. A place where they were not confronted by skinny loud young men, forever touching their crotches and nubile women who, despite the time of year, only ever wore clothes that covered their middle third plus a pair of stilettos and a clutch bag.

The owner could not have been happier. The over thirties were never any trouble and they spent. Not like the pre-loaded teens, the over thirties of Leigh had disposable income and as social status demanded, were happy to spend it.

"It's full of blokes," said Clarence Siddall.

"It's early," replied Leo Grant. "You know women, they like to make an entrance. To be watched to the bar and it gives the men a chance to neck a few beforehand."

Clarence Siddall wasn't exactly necking it but he was on his second gin and tonic. Both men stood either side of a round pub table. The day time furniture had been removed. They had their backs to the wall. Leo Grant looked at his disconsolate friend.

"C'mon it's Friday night, we are on the town and your HMI worries are no more."

"I didn't want the HMI inspecting Red Watch, that's all," he snapped. "Now, it's ten times worse. They think I've set them up. They think I want them sacked. They will, to a man, hate me."

"Did you set them up?"

"Jesus Christ, Leo. I am ambitious, driven you might say." He swilled his ice. "I know I can be over zealous and I've never seen eye to eye with the Unions but to conspire to have fire-fighters prosecuted, who do you think I am?"

"Then your conscience is clear and with regards to what people think, you can't do anything. You do your job and the rest will take care of itself."

In the meantime, the noise level had gone up a notch with "Hi's" and "mwahs" and "glad you could make it, what you having."

"Have you heard anything Leo, are the top floor saying anything, anything about me?"

"Right. I've heard nothing, okay. Now that's it for the night. Let's have a laugh. It's your round."

"Ok, but I'm going to the loo first."

He weaved his way back to Leo, carrying a house double in each hand. "Ah, this is my friend and associate, Clarence Sodall."

Leo saw the anger in his friend's eyes.

"Only joking, Siddall, Clarence Siddall. This is Violet and Clare," said an effusive Leo.

"Oh hallo, er can I get you a drink?"

"No, we are fine, thanks."

Leo Grant may have been an irritant to many of his colleagues but his ebullient nature was perfect in these situations. An awkward silence was an anathema to him. He bubbled, chuckled, tapped the side of his nose while giving a cheeky wink and described the mundane aspects of his life in forensic detail. He directed his verbal assault mainly at Violet whom to Clarence Siddall, Clare and the party at the next table's amazement seemed to be enjoying herself. Meanwhile.

"What do you do?"

"I'm a dental hygienist."

"How do you get into a job like that?"

"Started as a dental assistant."

He scanned the crowded bar for familiar faces. The last thing he needed was Eddie Hart to walk in. His gaze returned to their intimate group.

"Oh, do you enjoy it?"

"Yes, dental hygiene and therapy is important to our health in various ways but my biggest kick is soaking my latex gloves in chloroform and while the patient is out cold, I can rifle through their handbags or wallets."

The front door banged open and two men and women in high spirits bowled in. They were strangers to him.

"Oh that's interesting," he said, before the second part of her sentence penetrated his distracted mind. "What?"

"Look here, forgive me for being blunt, my friend and I come here most weeks for a few drinks and a laugh. We are not desperate and gagging for it and we are happy with our own company. If however, someone like Leo wants to have some fun and chat, then great. The last thing I want is to talk about work, my personal life, my ten-year-old son or my marital status, which more often than not is what I end up doing in here with blokes who want the detail before deciding if they are going to try and shag me. It's just a night out and a few drinks."

Clare's tirade focused his mind. He took a long pull on his gin and tonic, which hit him simultaneously in his head and stomach. His third drink of the night banished his anxiety.

"Sorry, tough week." He smiled.

"So'k."

"As anyone told you, you look like—"

"Annie Lennox? No."

"Has anyone told you, you look like Robert Redford?"

"No, never."

It was her turn to smile.

"Look, I know you don't want to talk about work but when you chloroform the patients, apart from robbing them, is there any sexual abuse?"

"Depends."

"On what?"

"How big their tits are."

Leo Grant stopped in mid-sentence when his wing man burst out laughing. *Excellent,* he thought. "Right, my round, girls and boys, what we all having?"

160

Chapter 40

The Red Watch returned for duty in sombre mood. The accusation of larceny hung heavy on the collective heart. The fresh bonhomie of a first day back was there but a thin carapace of its usual robust self. They carried out the mundane duties while trying to forget the theft. Sitting in a surgery while a doctor read with studied seriousness the possible life changing results from a worrying biopsy provided an apt simile.

Eddie asked his leading fire-fighters to join him in his room. Eddie sat on his desk. John Mullins chose the cot bed while Chris Everett decided to stand leaning against the lockers.

"It's not going to be an easy tour," said Eddie. "While we wait for an outcome if any." John was rolling a fag for later. He was the only Watch member who smoked.

"The sooner the better," he said.

Chris watched the long-practiced manufacture of the cigarette. "There's more Rizla than baccy in your roll ups. How long does an ounce last you?"

"A week, maybe more."

"Must be like dust after day five."

"A bit of lettuce, see, keeps it moist."

"Good idea, I prefer menthol."

"Didn't know you smoked."

"In the occasional joint. Anyway, do you think we should keep everyone busy, Eddie?"

"No, I think the opposite. We all need one another right now. It's the same after a nasty job. Talking among ourselves is best. Cathartic."

"I notice Clarence Siddall ain't around, fucking skate," said John, dropping his roll up in the pouch.

"I don't think we will see any senior officers until the police report their findings. They won't want to be seen jumping one way or the other," said Eddie.

"Just circle like fucking vultures," said John.

Eddie stood. "I wanted to say thanks to you both for your support. It ain't been easy, especially with Arthur off sick."

Chris smiled. "What else we gonna do? Its shit now but I think this will all blow over. I listened to all the statements and unless the old bill have something they are not sharing, I'd be amazed if they had enough evidence to hang it on one of us."

It was John's turn to stand. "I think you're right Chris but if it is one of our own, the police will have it easy cos I'll swing for the bastard, I swear."

"No, I think we can all agree it ain't one of us," said Eddie. "Let's do the routines and paper work and hope we get a few shouts."

Chris opened the door. "I'll start with the petty cash, surprise, surprise, it's a few pence out. I'll have a quick smoke then do the drill records."

"Thanks, chaps. I've got a couple of fire reports that need doing."

Chapter 41

Clarence Siddall was at SHQ. He sat patiently in DO's Gladstone's office, waiting for him to finish a long-winded phone call regarding a major restructuring of the Service. Having replaced the receiver in its cradle, he made notes.

His tongue ran back and forth over his bottom lip with juvenile concentration, revealing a set of small and very even teeth that could have been mistaken for dentures. Placing the pen across the pad in a theatrical attempt to protect his thoughts from espionage, he sat back in his chair.

"ADO. I have a few questions regarding this problem at your Station which are troubling me." The DO was not one to prevaricate.

It's my Station now, thought Clarence Siddall.

"Why did you take it on yourself to go to the incident where the theft took place when you had not been ordered by control and why did you remain and collect the necessary details, a job the Watch Officers should do?"

"Would you have any objection if I remove my jacket, sir? The sun through your window is directly on me."

"Yes, go on."

It was one of the reasons DO Gladstone like this office. It placed subordinates under his scrutiny in the spotlight. He knew it gave the ADO time to think and he appreciated the ploy. Clarence Siddall sat back down and pulled his tie below his Adam's apple.

"We have spoken in the past, Sir, about troublesome Watches. You are aware of the history we have with Red Watch, so I thought with the upcoming HMI visit looming on the horizon that some close order drill, so to speak was required. I thought it the right time to impose a degree of authority."

"Why had you not imposed you authority earlier? Months earlier."

"Yes Sir, you're right. I had been trying a lighter touch, guiding rather than ordering."

At the same time as saying it, Clarence Siddall was thinking what corporate drivel. He couldn't, however tell the effect it was having on his stony-faced boss.

"I'm the first to admit, Sir that approach had come up short." DO Gladstone raised an eyebrow.

"Ok but why offer to remain at the incident to do the job of the Watch Officers, a decision I may add has made you a suspect in the case. If I had my way, you would all be suspended."

Clarence Siddall ploughed on. "I wanted," he paused, searching for the right words. "To impose authority and at the same time, encourage a closer working relationship with Temporary Station Officer Eddie Hart, which I believed would be an advantage going forward."

"Arthur Church too clever for you, eh. Thought you'd try the more invidious method of command. Divide and rule. I like it."

He felt the ropes of the rack ease a little. "More the latter, Sir. I want to rule and do the best for the service."

"And for yourself. We all do."

The unabated sun poured through the window. A line of sweat ran down Clarence Siddall's back.

"Well, why not, agreeing with your methods, I can now give the Old Man a clearer picture and the rest of it, reports, etc. you handled well," he said begrudgingly. He was off the rack. The DO continued.

"He thinks and I fully support him on this that this is a prime opportunity, whatever the outcome, to sort this bunch out and you can be in the vanguard, ADO. There comes in all careers, pivotal moments. The disbanding of Red Watch Langden could be yours."

This is my pivotal moment, thought Clarence Siddall, here and now.

"I don't want that sir and I would be only too happy to talk to the Chief personally about it."

Divisional Officer Gladstone had always thought Clarence Siddall to be an ineffectual man. Someone to be used for one's own ends. To say the ADO's comment came as a surprise would be an understatement. The push and pull of it, he would consider later.

"Would you indeed, ADO? Perhaps you should tell me first."

"Firstly, I do not believe they stole the money. Nor may I add, did I. They may be a thorn in our side but thieves, they are not. I see this as a chance to build an effective working relationship between them and me. I want to gain their trust, Sir."

The DO got up from his desk and drew the blind across the window. The opaque light dropped the room temperature. Back at his desk, he lifted the receiver from its cradle and dialled a three-digit number.

"Ah Moira, yes hallo, fine thanks. No, no, ah yes, of course. I'll tell Amanda tonight, she will be pleased. Moira, is the Old Man available now for a quick chat?"

He looked at his note pad and refrained from doodling. "Excellent, I will be right up with ADO Clarence Siddall." He replaced the phone. "I know what you intend to say, roughly, so it's only right you know what I'm going to propose." The DO gestured to him to get up.

"If the Chief gives you your opportunity, then I'll support you. If one or more prosecutions for theft are successful, then you and I will systematically take Red Watch apart. Agreed?"

"Yes, Sir. Agreed."

For the Red, the day dragged on in a dispiriting manor. They drank tea, ran over the sequence of events, ate sandwiches at stand easy while talking about it. They concluded that John, Luke, Sam, Jim, Eddie and Clarence Siddall had all at some time been in the room and would have noticed something amiss going on. They had lunch and while eating a choice of a ham salad, a pork pie salad or just a salad, went over it again.

On the stroke of two, the bells went down. It was a hedgerow alight, a mundane job for the water tender. The main cause of the fire was a discarded or stolen moped. It was becoming the norm that Sam should run out the hose reel and extinguish the fire. The creamy flowers, leaves and thorny branches of the Hawthorn in close proximity to the bike were burnt and shrivelled.

The hedge bordered a farmer's field. John Mullins was full of tea. He would not be able to wait until they returned home. He lit a roll up, threw his tunic in the front of the cab and nipped behind the thicket for a Jimmy Riddle. Adam noticed his surreptitious departure and told Perry. They both stood behind Sam who stood in front of the fire.

Directly in line and partially hidden by charred hedgerow was pissing John. The well-practiced manoeuvre was over before Sam realised what had happened. Adam flung his arms about Sam, pinning him in a vice like grip. Perry simultaneously grabbed the hose reel branch, opened it up full throttle and directed a powerful jet through the hedge, hitting the Officer in charge of the water tender instantly in his exposed manhood. By the time John Mullins had screamed "bastards," and Sam had realised what had taken place, Adam and Perry were nowhere to be seen.

The soaking wet leading fire-fighter emerged from the bushes. "You put my fag out."

"I, I, it, it—"

"When we get back, I want a written report of your actions at this incident."

"I'm, it, I."

"Anyone ever told you that you talk like Donald duck shits."

"What?"

"All over the fucking place."

John walked past him to the rear of the appliance where Perry and Adam were looking meaninglessly at the pump dials. They were both doing their best to contain a snigger.

"Cunts."

Later that afternoon, when they had finished the volleyball of which Sam did not take part, John received the report he ordered earlier. He took it into the leading fire-fighter's room where Chris was closing in on the murderer.

"Look at this," said John.

"Bloody ell, talk about chapter and verse. Why did you make him do this?"

"Well, I expected four lines saying it weren't me, guv."

"He'll laugh about it one day. Well, he ain't grassed anyone up," said Chris.

"So we've learnt something if he ain't. Offered to buy me a pouch of tobacco."

"What did you say?"

"I told him I'm his boss not his potential bum bandit. No offence, Chris."

"None taken, John."

"C'mon, let's go home."

Chapter 42

The following day, Ray contacted three estate agents. He was excited to learn a possible selling price. He would then know what he could look for in London. A flat in a retirement complex would be nice, not too far from the Conservative club. He sat in his chair. Would he take it with him, probably not, a few pots and pans, the microwave?

His heart was light and for the first time, he was excited about the future. He had finished agreeing with the best part of the Daily Mail and his mind, not for the first time, went over the conversation with his son. The first part had been wounding for them both. The second, at the cemetery, brought relief and solace for him, he hoped it was mutual.

They had stood for a while, looking at the headstone in silent reverence. Someone had hung a dream catcher and wind chimes in a nearby tree. Eddie commented how close the grave was to Jim's house. The head stone said, 'Evelyn Hart, her dates then Beloved wife and mother. Taken too soon.'

"Well, I've read more flowery citations," said Eddie. "Can't help thinking if you meant the sentiment."

"Let's stop son shall we, anyway you had gone AWOL, I didn't know what to have inscribed. Something from Larkin perhaps."

"Well, perhaps you can have it added, I don't know."

Bending to pull a weed, he wondered if this was the last time they would be together as a family. "Shall we?"

They sat on the bench.

"Where did you go? All those weekends."

"London, where else. I only went for the day initially. First train out last home and not every weekend cos of work, then, Phyllis."

"Pardon?"

"Her name was Phyllis. She worked in the garment trade. Started going to the club with her husband and after her marriage went south and her husband north, she kept coming. It started when she offered me a bed after missing the last train."

"So all those weekends, with her."

"Yes, son."

"Why didn't you just leave?"

"If only life was so simple, son. You see, I stayed in my marriage but it didn't work. Her husband left because it didn't work. She was bitter, not with me, she even admired me, and she couldn't reconcile herself to a failed marriage. She definitely never wanted another."

"Are you still together?"

"No, she died three years ago, pancreatic cancer. Terrible. I hear from her daughter occasionally."

"Was she the daughter you never had, always wanted?"

"No son, I told you fatherhood is alien to me. Uncle Ray when she was young, not in a cosy avuncular way. We were uninterested in one another."

"Fucking hell."

"I liked her, good kid. She wasn't flesh and blood though. She wasn't you."

"Did you love her mother?"

"No, son. We were like two peas in pod. Same humour, same politics, same likes and dislikes but not love. I think I'm incapable of it. Eros, maybe."

In vain, he waited for his son to see the humour.

"It made the living apart easy."

"You really want to go and live in London."

"Yes, I do, son. Maybe that's my true love. Tired of London, tired of life, eh."

"Samuel Johnson?"

"No, Ray Hart."

This time, his son smiled.

"It's changed so much since your day. Culturally, especially in your neck of the woods."

"Ah I see, so your assumption is Tory equals racist."

"Well to be blunt, yea."

"That's where you are like your mother. Dogmatic. As bright as she was and she could argue me under the table, politically she lacked nuance. Right was wrong and she would brook no argument."

He watched his son pluck a grass stem, inspect it and place it Clint Eastwood style in the corner of his mouth.

"London has always been a melting pot. Black people, Jews, French Huguenots and now, what Bangladeshi, I don't know. Don't care. I'll have a bus pass. In no time, I could be in the city or the Woolwich Ferry for a ride south of the river. The West End, oh I love Soho, especially early mornings as it wakes for a new day."

"I like Broadway in the mornings. So we have something in common. Did Mum know?"

"No, our weekends apart were our own affair. I knew she had trips with her girlfriends, she knew I had London. It was the one part of our marriage that worked."

"Not the only part, Dad."

He looked at his son.

"Between the two of you, you provided me with a good, safe and loving home."

It would have been the perfect moment to hug his son, instead he decided on a gesture less demonstrative. Eddie smiled at his father's peace offering, reached out and shook his hand. An old lady bent over her walking stick, came to rest in the shade of the tree. She heard the wind chime and with difficulty, looked up.

"Stuff and nonsense," she chirruped.

She looked over at Ray and Eddie sitting on the bench then at Eve's headstone. Silently, she mouthed the dates.

"It gets easier, boys."

"Would you like to sit?" asked Ray.

"No, mustn't keep him waiting," she nodded in the direction where her husband lay. "Good day to you."

"Bye."

Eddie gazed at his mother's grave. "What will survive of us is love."[6]

"Larkin?" asked Ray.

"Yea for the headstone."

"Perfect."

At the station, another day of ennui was drawing to a close.

---

[6] *An Arundel Tomb* by Phillip Larkin

"No news is good news," said Ken, placing the last tray of tea for the day on the mess table. If he was honest with himself, being completely in the clear, he was beginning to get the arse with the whole situation.

"Can't be much longer," said Billy.

"Fuckin 'ope not," said Ken.

"Why, what you worried about?" asked Perry.

"Oh well, I'm worried for you lot. Here, some suggestive biscuits I took off the pumps emergency feeding. They are out of date."

"You fucking spoil us."

"Is there a better mess manager?"

Eddie was absent. He was taking a shower, keen to get away as soon as possible. He had managed to get an appointment at short notice with his counsellor. The Station Officer on the Green came in half hour early for him. Eddie walked into the mess.

"Night, lads."

"Oi, where you going all spruced up?"

"Got a date?"

"Yea."

"Do we know her?"

"No."

"Well, spill."

"If you must know, I'm going to see my shrink."

"Fucking ell, gonna be a long night."

"See ya."

The banter with the Watch hid Eddie's turmoil. Trying to come to terms with his father's recent revelations, though enlightening, was causing him an angst that needed working through. Things had to be unpicked. He timed his arrival to perfection, going straight into the counsellor's room.

"So Mr Hart, how are we?"

"Brilliant fucking brilliant."

"Okay. I'm not sure that sounds brilliant but let's see, we have been talking about your mother. Would you like to continue or—?"

"No."

Eddie helped himself to water.

"Then what would you like or need, to talk about?"

"My father."

Around the same time, Clarence Siddall met Clare for a drink in The Broadway Thorpe Bay. The road name differentiated from its counterpart in Leigh by its article was in other ways similar. A strip perfectly suited to the pre-prandial delights of cafe society. It was handy too. Clarence lived five minutes' walk away and Clare ten.

"What would you like?"

"Well, it's a school night so better just make it a vodka tonic."

He checked himself, waiting for the punch line that never arrived.

"Just a single, and tell them not to drown it, oh and no ice, just lemon or lime."

He returned with the drinks and a shallow tray containing olives of varying hues.

"It's so nice to see you again. Thanks for coming. I had such a good time the other night."

"Eventually."

"Yes, sorry about that. I wasn't in the room so to speak at the start of the evening but," a shyness overcame him. "You changed that."

They both took a drink. She pushed the olives towards him. "Do you like them?"

"Not really. They're okay."

"I'd rather eat my own placenta and it's a good excuse to price hike the drinks. I haven't been in here before, you?"

"No."

"I don't mean to pry but you have a son, I seem to remember."

"Yes, Harvey, my Harv. Ten and you're not prying."

"It's just, the other night when you said what you would and wouldn't talk about."

"That was the other night. Time and place and all that. This is different. We are not going to sit here and talk about the economy, at least I'm not and if you do, I'm off. You tell me what it's like in a burning building and rescuing cats from trees and I'll tell you about the inside of people's mouths and if you're lucky, my favourite film."

The drinks were sipped reluctantly to their conclusion while they provided one another with their intimate curriculum vitae. A member of the bar staff wiped the next table and asked if they wanted anything else. It interrupted the flow.

"Oh, is that the time, I better go. Vi is looking after Harv."

"Can I see you again?"

"Yea, somewhere else though. Pub maybe or the pictures." Elation didn't do justice to his feeling at that moment. "You really do look a lot like Annie Lennox."

"Yea that's why I keep my hair like this. I like the compliment and you really don't look like Robert Redford. He's not my type anyway."

"Oh who is," he said, fishing.

"Hmm, someone like you or Danny DeVito. You two are like twins, I bet only your mother could tell you apart."

He had never been so offended and so happy at the same time. She got up, kissed him on the cheek and left. The bar staff was still close at hand.

"Excuse me."

"Yes, sir."

"Can I have a large gin and tonic please?"

"Certainly."

"And would you mind changing these for some peanuts please."

"Olives not to your liking, sir."

"No, my girlfriend and I, she just left, we don't like them."

Clarence Siddall looked at the chair she had been sitting on and the glass she had held. *Hmmm, my girlfriend,* he thought.

Chapter 43

The following morning Eddie rose early, ran to the gym and gave the punch bag 'what for' then ran home again. The 'what for' the heavy bag received was different than of late. More akin to someone wanting to tone rather than commit murder. He felt a brightness of spirit, a man who had been deafened by a concussive force that could hear again.

He finally understood his father for the first time in his life. It may not have been what he wanted to hear but it was far better than the not knowing. Of course, he should not try to stop him moving back to London. He wasn't emigrating. He had to let him go. The counsellor agreed.

His mother also, release her from his own purgatory and remember her for what she was. The biggest influence and love, of whatever kind, in his life. Then work, he knew he could handle it now plus the longer it went on, the more confident he was, there was no case to answer.

He cooked a fry up. He wanted red meat but settled for three rashers of smoked back, a Cumberland sausage, fried egg easy over and tomatoes. He would worry about the smell in his flat later. He sat inside, not trusting the thieving gulls to have it away with his succulent greasy breakfast.

Afterwards, he cleaned up immediately, opened the windows, patio doors and turned on the fragrant plug in. He wanted coffee but a pressing need to get going prevented him. He needed to talk to someone urgently. He liked the new talkative self so picking up the phone, he dialled.

"Hello Nev, it's Eddie Hart, hello, Nev are you at work this morning, no it's you I want to talk to. Good, good, I'll be right over, say thirty minutes."

Nev was going through the motions, practicing a few strangle holds. *If he thinks he's coming here to tell me he wants my wife, then he'll be unconscious before he finishes the sentence,* he thought. *Got to admire his balls though and they are gonna get kicked up behind his ears. Stop it Nev, stay calm, then he won't see it coming.*

I'll punch him up the throat if he tries anything, thought Eddie as he drove to his meeting. *That takes down most men in my experience.*

I'll start with all I want to do is talk Nev, he'll understand. Eddie rang the front doorbell. The door was opened immediately by a looming Nev.

"Hallo Nev, I just want—"

"Go through the side gate to the back garden."

"Can I come?"

"No, side gate." He closed the door.

Eddie stuck his head around the corner of the house to see Nev already sitting at a garden table not dissimilar to his father's. He had a steaming mug in his left hand.

"May I?"

Nev nodded at the other seat.

"What you got, tea?"

"Yea."

"Nice."

"I've run out of milk."

"I can drink it black."

"I've run out of tea."

With the niceties over, Eddie got straight to the point.

"I've known you, Jane and Charlotte for a long time now. Jane since we were kids."

"I know."

"Jane meant a lot to my mum and Charlotte, she was so pleased she got into university."

"What you come here for, Eddie?"

Nev's interjection made him realise he was waffling.

"Ok Nev, since Eve's death, I've been in a shit place and one person who has really helped me has been Jane. You are not naive or a fool, Nev and thinking back over the last months then I'm surprised I never heard from you, shall I say. That was it though Nev, help. Nothing else and I wanted to come here today to say that and to say thank you."

"Like I said on the phone, she ain't here."

"No, to you, Nev. I want to say thank you to you for your consideration and understanding."

"Don't know if I've been any of that, just not a believer of imposing my wishes on my wife. What good does that do?"

"Look, it's obvious I've caused problems and I don't want to. I'm here to say I'll get out of your hair." Eddie laughed.

"What's so funny?"

"Sorry Nev, out of your hair, Jane, haircut. It doesn't matter." Eddie got up. "I think I should go and let you be. Both of you. I'll get the Barnet cut elsewhere." Nev stood.

Fuck me, he's big, thought Eddie.

"Can I send you a voucher for that swanky restaurant in Old Leigh, it's got great reviews."

"No thanks, find your own woman and take her there. Thanks though for coming and saying what you said."

"Ok Nev, I'll see myself out."

"How's your father?"

"Good thanks, moving to London. Selling the house. Anyway."

Nev pursed his lips and nodded.

"Here, come through the house, it's quicker."

Chapter 44

The first night shift brought no respite to the collective anxiety. Mundane tasks were performed in silence and the game of volleyball was played by two teams going through the motion. Ken had decided on a curry to spice up the evening and it was partially consumed when the bells went down.

Both pumps were ordered to three vehicles involved in a collision, persons trapped. The location was the notorious Barge Aground roundabout on the A128, London bound carriageway. Perry and Sam were fully rigged, sitting in the rear of the pump.

"Unless the road is completely blocked, the old bill will be keen to keep a lane open," Perry was telling Sam.

"Both machines will fend off to protect us from through traffic. Make sure you don't wander into the open lane. Stay with me unless Eddie or John gives you a job."

The three cars involved were at the junction of the A128 and the High Street. An elderly man in a Toyota Cherry coming from town had driven onto the A road straight into the path of a Mercedes. The T bone impact snapped his neck at C3, killing him instantly. A Ford Granada had hit the Merc up the arse.

"Dark and Light Green were already in attendance. We guessed you would want the roads shut, Eddie."

"Yea, it's still busy. What we got?"

"One brown bread. Old boy. City slicker in the Merc with a broken nose. Middle aged couple in the Granada, don't know really."

"Cheers, Dark."

"Ok, run out a hose reel and put up the lighting mast."

Eddie went straight to the Cherry. Looking through the shattered window, he saw the elderly man covered in a thousand tiny cubes of glass. His head at an unnatural angle. A moment, a lapse of concentration had cost him dear. Eddie thought he recognised him but couldn't think from where.

John joined him.

"We'll have to cut the door off to get the old boy out, John." John looked in the car.

"No rush."

"Nah, no rush."

The city slicker was moaning like fuck. Out of his vehicle, he was holding a handkerchief to his face and complaining loudly to Light Green about the idiot who pulled out right in front of him. He must be blind. Hope he's insured, I'm going to need plastic surgery.

"Do you feel dizzy or feint?"

"No, I feel bloody angry."

"Have you been drinking?"

"For the love of Christ. I'm the victim here."

The fire-fighters knew not to ignore the noisy ones but make them low priority. It was the quiet ones that demanded attention. Eddie surveyed the scene. His crew from the rescue pump were busy with the door of the Toyota. Light Green was having his patience tested. Dark Green was taking measurements and Adam, Perry and Sam had surrounded the Granada where not a lot of action was taking place. He went over.

"They ain't trapped, Eddie. He's complaining of chest pains and she weren't wearing her seat belt," said Adam.

"She's got the biggest egg on her forehead that I've seen in a long time."

"Okay," replied Eddie, "these two are the priority for the paramedics."

Perry and Sam were on their haunches, talking to the couple. Perry asking casual first aid questions. Sam listening.

"Look at this," said Adam discreetly. He showed Eddie the windscreen of the Granada still intact. Where the woman's head had hit the screen, there was a small tuft of hair, on the outside.

"I reckon she hit it with such force, the laminate opened up for a fraction of a second and as she went back into her seat, it ripped her hair out."

Eddie looked in the car. Sure enough, the woman had an enormous lump on her hair line. A hair line that was interrupted by this incongruous bald patch. The couple sat in polite acquiescence, awaiting the attention of the medical team, comforted by Perry's reassuring tone.

"We also disconnected the battery," said Adam.

The paramedics, seeing Eddie's white helmet went straight to him. "Evening, couldn't get through the traffic, what we got?"

"Evening, have a look at these two first, if you want the roof off, let me know."

Sam stood up. His thighs had started to burn from the squat position he'd assumed five minutes earlier. He watched Eddie scan the crash site and wished he could suggest an action or idea that would impress him. John Mullins joined them at the Granada. "Alright," he said.

"Yea, I think we got it covered until they remove the casualties and body," Eddie replied, "and the broken nose has finally shut up."

"I think Light got fed up with him and told him he's killed an old man. Anyway the door's off, oh and I just heard Clarence Siddall is on his way."

"Fuck sake!" Exclaimed Adam, "if he comes here and starts dishing it out tonight, I'm letting him have it, both barrels."

Eddie smiled, "well, don't give him any ammo."

"What?"

"Put your helmet on."

"I'll get it," said Sam.

The drivers of front-line appliances would leave their helmets on the engine cowling that separated the two front seats. It was the driver's job to employ the pump when in attendance. The driver engages a power take off in the cab before running to the rear of the appliance to pump operate, sometimes grabbing his helmet as he goes, sometimes not.

Adam's helmet still sat in the cab between the seats.

"It's OK, I'll—"

Sam was already on his way, keen to do anything to help the team. He ran around to the driver's door, arriving at the same time as the young man on motorbike.

Eddie and Adam weren't facing in the direction of the lorry when the impact happened. What they heard wasn't very loud apart from the high whine of the bike's engine and the scraping metal sliding across the road. What they saw as they turned was a leather clad figure hit the Armco on the central reservation and Sam lying in the road.

Eddie got to him first. Sam looked like a discarded doll. He had blood coming from his nose and ears and his left leg was wrong.

"Sam, Sam, can you hear me?"

Eddie saw the black boots in his peripheral vision. He looked up. It was Dark Green. "You opened the fucking road."

"No Eddie, he's come through on his own."

Sam was mouthing something Eddie couldn't make out.

"Get the paramedics over here now and turn that fucking motor bike off," shouted Eddie. He took his helmet off and got down close to Sam. "You're gonna be OK, Sam."

Sam wasn't in pain, he had this strong feeling that he wanted to urinate and knew from his training that his pelvis was likely smashed. *I might be dying,* he thought.

"Sam, can you hear me?"

It was a whisper, no more. Eddie had his ear close to Sam's mouth and despite the mayhem around him, heard clearly what Sam had to say.

The rest of the night was conducted underwater. The members of Red Watch could hear themselves breath, their voices muffled, their thoughts obscure. In the months ahead, when they would sit around the mess table with mugs of tea in front of them, none would be able to recall the rest of that night. It had ended at the moment of impact.

Chapter 45

Jane had come home in a huff. Mary had quit.

"I thought she lacked potential, as you put it," said Nev.

"She lacked most things, not nerve though. She's off to Brighton evidently, with her boyfriend."

"When?"

"In the morning. Working her notice, apparently an alien concept."

"Did she give a reason?"

"Yea, her fella has got a job, bar work, and she will easily get something with the summer season starting. Her words, not mine."

Jane looked about the living room. "Where are my slippers?"

"I washed them. They are on the line."

"Nev! My feet do not smell."

"Your feet may not but they did. How long you had that pair?"

"Can't remember but I love 'em, comfy, reliable," she said with some consideration.

"I think you look forward to coming home to them more than me."

"Ooh, an evening in me slippers knocks you into a cocked hat."

"Shall we order in tonight, I fancy Chinese," he said.

Jane went to the kitchen draw and pulled out a menu. She sat next to her husband on the sofa. I thought I was getting somewhere with her recently and I'm bloody busy at the moment. Nev took the folded card, knowing he was about to add to his wife's woes. "Eddie came here."

She looked at Nev, wondering if she heard right. "When?"

"This morning."

"Go on."

Nev relayed the sequence of events and conversation he had with Eddie. Jane did not interrupt. Her feelings, at first matter of fact, gradually overwhelmed her as the import of what had taken place in her garden that morning sunk in. She looked through the patio doors, imagining the scene. Nev looked idly inside the menu then at the back of it as one does at a funeral program.

"Tea, love," he said.

"No thanks."

Nev put his arm around his wife.

"Carry on with his hair. I don't mind and Charlotte will expect to see him from time to time."

"No Nev, he won't come back in the shop. I know him."

He's gone again, she thought.

"Oh, he also said Ray is selling up, going back to London."

She leaned against her husband, feeling his long arm envelope her. This huge solid rock of a man. "I love you, Nev."

"I know, love. Boring, fussy old me. Who'd have thought? Couldn't believe it when you said yes." He turned to face her. "Still can't. Are you going to be alright?"

Jane broke hold and went to the breakfast bar where she plucked a couple of tissues. "Yea, I'll be fine." She blew. "It's just, well, since Eve's death." She struggled with her thoughts. "It's just not fair, that's all." She pulled out a stool from under the counter, sat down and looked at her husband.

"Ray lost his wife, Ed lost his mother and I lost them all."

Chapter 46

Eddie spent the following day visiting people. He started at the hospital where Sam was in intensive care. He explained who he was and asked to see his colleague. His request was declined, he was informed that his condition was stable. He went to see his father and told him of the incident in detail.

Ray understood his son's need and listened attentively. He did not proffer an opinion. He could see Eddie working through the sequence of events in his head that was providing his own reassurance. He knocked on Dark Green's door and over coffee, apologised for the way he spoke to him at the incident.

"No problem Eddie, one of your own was down. I'd have been the same."

Then after much deliberation, he went to see Sam's parents. He had important matters to discuss so they could all move forward. After a fraught meeting, it was clear he had to see someone else and the sooner he contacted her, the better.

Chapter 47

The second night shift started in much the same way as thousands before. The appliance checks were carried out, the tea made, the Watch gathered in the mess. The mood, however, was unique.

Never before had they nearly lost one of their own and he wasn't out of the woods yet. Sam's situation brought home to them the stark reality of the job and its risks. They had witnessed the troubled look on the faces of their loved ones as they relayed the events of the previous night. The inherent danger of their profession made tangible by a split-second mistake.

Clarence Siddall and Eddie were in the office, the door was closed.

"Leon spends more time in that office than he does with us," said Luke. Harryoo looked at Luke.

"What's the point?" he said.

"What?"

"Leon."

"I just like the name. Think it's a cool nickname. Better than Eddie."

"Right, lads." Eddie walked into the mess room, followed by the ADO. "The guvnor wants to talk to us." Both men joined the Watch around the table.

"Gentlemen, you know what this is about, so I'll cut to the chase. Sam will be in intensive care for the foreseeable future. He is in an induced coma because of swelling to his brain. His pelvis and left femur are shattered and will need extensive surgery.

"He is stable and because of his age and general health, fitness, etc. they are confident of his recovery. To what extent, obviously no one can say at this stage. Again, as you all know, the motorcyclist died at the scene. His next of kin have been informed and apart from inquest that's the end of the matter as far as the police are concerned.

"I spent the day with ADO Leo Grant, at the site and here, going over every aspect of the incident with regards to command and control. We both agreed that

183

procedures were carried out correctly and Sam, when going to the cab of the rescue pump to retrieve a fire ground radio went to the wrong side of the lorry, thereby exposing himself to the danger of through traffic. The fact that the road was closed and the biker decided he was going to weave through is a salutary lesson for us all. Any questions?"

Adam raised a half-hearted hand and spoke. "It was my—"

Eddie cut across him.

"I know what you're going to say, Adam and it's irrelevant."

"What's that?" asked Clarence Siddall.

"Adam is going to say, guv that I asked him to get the radio and Sam in his eagerness ran to get it instead."

"You're not to feel guilty about that, Adam," said the ADO, "on small decisions rest the most significant outcomes. Right now for the good news."

Some sat back in their chairs, they looked at one another, concerned that the ADO was being ironic and this was the end of the Red Watch as they knew it.

"Miss," he looked at piece of paper in his hand. "Miss Lucy Holding."

Lucifer, thought Chris.

"She has dropped her accusation of theft regarding the £1000." Clarence Siddall smiled. No one spoke immediately. Ken broke the silence.

"Phew that's a relief. The stress I've been under. Takes its toll that kind of thing. Can we sue for wrongful, you know."

There were a few incredulous expressions around the table. Harryoo decided he loved Ken more than ever.

"I didn't think you were at that incident, Ken."

"No, guv'nor. I mean, can the watch sue collectively like?"

"When did you know and what exactly has gone on?" asked John Mullins.

"I received a call from PC Kaminski within the last hour. She phoned him direct." Clarence Siddall looked again at the paper in his hand. "I made a few notes. He said she apologised profusely and would he pass on the same sentiment to us here. It seems she had a one-night stand recently. The man was also a mutual friend of her best girlfriend."

"Probably doing them both."

The ADO looked up but missed the remark's origin. "Please," he continued. "Miss Holland was told by the girlfriend that the man had been in their local, showing off an expensive watch that he had recently purchased. When asked how he got the money, he laughed and said, for services rendered." It was Clarence Siddall's turn to smile.

"The two women put two and two together and came to the same conclusion. What about wasting police time?" Suggested Jim.

"Well, the initial accusation was genuine and the police appreciated her candid disclosure. So I guess not. Anyway, I have phone calls to make so if you will excuse me, oh and before I go, you should know counselling is available should you feel the need to talk to a professional about anything. It is completely confidential. The number is in our directory. No one need know. Thank you."

The bells went down. All three appliances were ordered to the ward seven of the mental health unit. While proceeding to the hospital, Billy Butler remembered it was Sam's very first shout and how keen and excited he was. It saddened him to see the empty place next to him.

Upon arrival, they were met by a scrum of people and smoke issuing from a window. The kitchen pantry fire while substantial was easily contained. It did involve the evacuation of the ward and extensive firefighting procedures. It was three hours before they were all back at the station.

Eddie said, "Come in." It was Adam. "Alright, mate?"

"No, Eddie. I'm not and you know why." He plonked himself down on the made-up cot bed.

"Adam, I get it but you didn't ask him to get your helmet. That was Sam's decision and he made a mistake. Perry has told me he went through the fend off procedures with him while preceding. Whether he went for your helmet or a fire ground radio is irrelevant. He made the mistake and the last thing we all need now is further complications."

Adam seemed unconvinced.

"You are one of the best fire-fighters I've ever worked with, Adam and the fact that you're hurting over this is the mark of a good man. Sam won't blame you. He'll be OK. The theft accusation is behind us and this Watch is going to get back to normal. Trust me."

"Thanks, Eddie. I appreciate it." Opening the door, he turned and asked. "Do you want a cuppa?"

"Of course and Adam that counselling, it's not for me to say but think about it."

"Nah thanks Eddie, I think I just had it."

Chapter 48

The dry spell showed no sign of abating. Daffodils around town had put on a good show, now was the time to retreat and store their goodness in the earth for next year. The Labour Party were confident of a good showing in the upcoming local elections. One of their candidates was a fire officer serving in the town.

The fire service were riding high with the public following an article that featured Sam. One of Langden's finest who put their lives at risk to save others. Eddie didn't get to see him for three days. When he did, Sam was still in intensive care. He was conscious.

"Well, you're making good progress. I would have brought flowers if I knew you were awake." Sam gave a weak smile.

"They are not allowed. Thanks for coming."

"I tried before but you know how it is."

"Have you seen my parents?"

"Yep and your sister. I get the feeling I'm not your mother's favourite person."

"What because—"

"Yea, I was in charge, didn't look after you."

"She not going to do anything, pursue it, I mean."

"No, your father, lovely man, was very understanding and reassuring. I'm in the clear. How do you feel?"

"I don't. Can't feel a thing. That'll be the morphine, I guess."

"The doctors are confident there's no paralysis, smashed up a bit though, metal pins, more ops."

"What a bitch."

Suddenly, he was back at the barn fire. Sitting next to Eddie, drinking tea amid a bucolic ruin. He remembered his boss drawing a line in the earth with a small stick.

"I overstepped the mark."

"You went around the wrong side."

There was a communion between the two men in the silence that followed. A nurse came and took readings.

"Eddie. Eddie Hart, right?"

"That's me."

"You play football with my Wayne."

"Oh yea."

Eddie's recall was instant. There was only one Wayne. "Played. Not anymore. Too old."

"You look fit enough to me."

Eddie smiled.

"Say hi."

"I will."

Alone again. Sam was first to speak. "How is the rest of the Watch?"

"They are good. Happy you are going to be OK, over the moon the charges have been dropped. They will all be up to see you over the coming days."

"Dropped?"

"Yea, she realised a boyfriend had taken it."

Sam tried to turn his head to look directly at Eddie but a whirling dizziness stopped him. "I'm not coming back, am I?"

"No, Sam."

"You were wrong."

"About what?"

"Me, senior officer material."

A tear ran over Sam's temple into his ear. Eddie considered his reply.

"I remember sitting in a lecture many moons ago. The old boy, a scientist, wanted to inject some humour into proceedings. You must have experienced it at Uni. The triangle of fire, those basic scientific laws by which you fight your foe have been re-evaluated, he said. Nothing is immutable in our world. It is now a square. Oxygen, heat, fuel and a senior officer. Remove any one and the fire goes out."

He leaned forward, forearms on his knees.

"I reckon I was right, you were dopey enough."

Chapter 49

It was a ten-minute drive from the hospital to his father's. Before pulling away, he saw a porter whom he had spoken with on the night of the fire. He dropped his window.

"How is it? Ward seven."

"Chaos, never thought a small fire could have such a knock on effect and the smoke damage, fucking ell, more of a problem than the shit that burnt. We have got a specialist firm in to get it off the walls, nightmare."

"No one got hurt though."

"Nah, have a good'un."

The back door was open. Eddie walked into the living room. There were boxes strewn about. "Blimey, you don't waste any time. How are you?"

"I'm good, thanks son. I can't believe what I'm getting for this place. Young Romanian couple. What do you think of this, over sixties only, no communal lounge, which doesn't bother me but nice gardens by the look of it?"

Ray passed the literature to his son. Eddie scanned it and thought he had never seen his father this happy. It was infectious.

"Two beds."

"Yea so you can stay."

"Stay."

"Yea, overnight if you have one too many in the club."

"I take it you mean the Conservative club."

"Yea of course. It's just a club. It won't kill ya."

"No but if word got back Leon Trotsky was drinking with the devil, well."

"Leon Trotsky!"

"Doesn't matter."

"Here, son. You wanted this."

He placed the small collie dog in his hand. "Thanks, Dad."

"If it goes according to plan, I'll have a few bob over. So I'm gonna get Mum's headstone re-done. What was the phrase you suggested?"

"What will survive of us is love."

"That's it. Perfect."[7]

---

[7] *An Arundel Tomb* by Phillip Larkin

Chapter 50

Arthur Church returned to work. He sat in the mess and was keen to hear everything. The Watch responded, all chipping in like a class trying to please teacher. Ken asked Gretchen to make chocolate sponge pudding and chocolate custard for dessert. It was Arthur's favourite.

"Fucking crawler," said Harryoo, loading the dishwasher.

"Can't do enough for a good guvner," came the reply.

To a man, they had visited Sam. They knew with his injuries that he would not return, so were busy with a county wide collection and as Billy suggested, a station dance perhaps in aid of his recovery.

"What was he like?" asked Arthur.

"Nice young man," said Ken.

"Officer material." Perry.

"Senior officer material." Chris.

"Bit plumy but fitted in." John.

"I thought he was Delphic." Luke.

"He thought you was a cunt." Adam.

"And," said Harryoo, "it makes you the sprog again so cut along and help Gretchen with stand easy."

"I've brought milk," said Kay. "I noticed we were getting low. Jane, I know I've been here five minutes but have you ever considered a computer booking system. Easier and clearer."

"No but let's see, shall we?"

Jane's first customer was in five minutes. She prepared her work station. *Still can't believe my luck,* she thought. When things couldn't get worse, in walked Kay. Wanted a job, doing a B Tech at college one day a week, never had to be told to do anything once, let alone twice, bright and so personable.

The phone rang. Jane smiled as she listened to Kay's professional manner. "One minute please, sir."

She walked over to Jane. "It's a man by the name of Eddie. He would like to speak with you."

"Oh, tell him not now, thanks Kay."

"Certainly, should I give a reason?"

Jane placed her scissors in front of the mirror. "Yes, tell him that you are new here and was not aware that after much consideration, the salon is moving in a different direction and no longer intends to cut men's hair."

The water tender had the one call. Eddie, now a Sub Officer again, was in charge. It was to a woman locked out, baby inside. Mum was waiting for them outside the ground floor maisonette. She was dressed completely in black. Her hair, mascara and lipstick were also black. Her face was adorned with piercings.

"I just stepped out and it closed behind me." Eddie could hear the baby crying.

"He's in the hall in his buggy, we were going out." She pointed to a first-floor window.

"Looks closed but it ain't. It's broken."

"I'll get the triple ex," said Billy.

"It might seem an odd question but can you prove this is your place."

"I can when we get in."

Within two minutes, Billy opened the front door. There in the hall was a black buggy and the crying infant. He was dressed in black. The only nod to the opposite shade of black was the phrase across his little chest. 'Get your tits out' it said.

Once in his mother's arms, his cries became a whimper. "He needs feeding. Do you still want ID?"

"No, that's alright, you get him fed."

Chapter 51

"You OK?" asked Arthur, "You seem quiet today. Pissed off you're no longer in charge."

They were in Arthur's office. He was keen to hear Eddie's account of the last few weeks.

"No, no, Arthur on the contrary. I'm really glad you are back and next time you go sick, I want prior warning because I'm going sick too."

"How were Chris and John, supportive?"

"Couldn't have been more so. In fact, all the Watch have been great. I just don't think I'm cut out for leadership, especially when the shit hits, plus I've had plenty going on outside the job as well."

"How you been doing apropos your mum?"

"One good thing, about this recent episode is that everything for me came to a head at once. I really feel, apart from something today, like I've turned a corner."

"I'm pleased for you and on a selfish note, when Eddie Hart is happy, this Watch is truly happy."

"Fuck me, Arthur. I'm welling up here," he said, laughing.

Arthur looked to the floor and smiled. "Anyway, anything I need to know?"

"No but I want to know, would you have let the police interview the Watch?"

"Hmmm, interesting."

Chapter 52

After work, Eddie drove to Chalkwell and parked near the train station. He walked along the front towards Westcliff. It was a beautiful evening. The air was still and the sea the colour of blue steel. The small floating craft had their bows pointing towards the North Sea.

At the Arches, he saw Clarence Siddall sitting in front of the same place where as fire-fighters, they used to have a drink after work.

"Thanks for coming."

"I couldn't resist. I'm intrigued."

Eddie sat down and a young girl approached the table. "Er, a bottle of your coldest beer, please."

She started to list them.

"Surprise me."

"I'll have the same," said Clarence.

"The tide is on its way in," said Eddie.

"How was your day?"

"One shout, lock out, and Arthur's back so pretty good thanks. Yours?"

"Well despite being my day off, I still got a call from Gladstone. He asked after Sam said he had put in his collection and wanted me to arrange a visit for the Chief to see Sam in hospital and he wants me in attendance."

"Why's that?"

"Well evidently, he's pleased with how I've managed things recently." The two bottles of beer arrived. "I'm sure the irony is not lost on you, Eddie."

Eddie took a swig, his eyes followed two attractive women as they promenaded. "So I guess what you're saying is you got out the shit smelling of roses."

"Not a phrase I would use but yea. And this meeting. This is going to be difficult for me, Eddie but I need to talk to you, I want to apologise. Everything that has happened over these last few weeks, not just work I may add has made me re-evaluate my career and relationships. I was going to," it was his turn to take a swig. "I was going to try and bring the Red in line, please the top floor and thereby advance my career. There I've said it."

"I don't understand, bring us in line."

"The Watch ain't popular with the Chief Eddie especially Arthur. You know how it is Eddie, they deal with misdemeanours, fights, theft, even women on the station without breaking stride. Politics, well that is different. Politics are dangerous. It threatens. It threatens them. The HMI was my chance to show the boss how I could manage the most difficult situations. It wasn't long before it quickly unravelled and I would have done anything to get out of it. I didn't set the watch up with the alleged theft but that's exactly what it looked like. I was so relieved when that woman withdrew the accusation. Then there's me and you. It was going from bad to worse. I know I've been distant."

"Fucking distant!"

"I know, I know but our relationship was turning into outright hatred. I don't want that. So I asked you here tonight away from work to say sorry."

"I don't hate you, Clarence. I just don't understand. We used to come here after work for a beer. We came here after rescuing that kid from the river. I remember you still had mud behind your ear and if I must say, your reluctance to shower was a bit odd. You would never have got that muck off at the sink. I thought we were mates."

"Would you like another drink?" asked the young girl.

"Yea, same again please," said Eddie, without consultation. Eddie considered Clarence's apology while drinking his beer.

"It's been going on for a lot longer than you wanting to prove something with the HMI visit. Since you came to take charge of Langden, you have been cold, aloof and authoritarian with me in a way I thought was ridiculous. I hid my feelings behind an angry demeanour but it has hurt, Clarence."

He paused. "Look, I never got on really well with my father."

"Tell me about it," said Clarence.

"So I summoned the courage recently to ask him what I had done, prepared for whatever was to come. Well, I thought I was but anyway it ended positively, so I'm asking you the same question. What have I done, Clarence?"

On the other side of the road, a toddler dropped his ice cream and started to cry. The parents fussed over him.

"Shame," said Clarence, "is one powerful emotion. I guess it started when I thought my father was ashamed with me. I felt shame throughout my school years for reasons I won't go into here. I felt shamed when he chose my sister to run the family business but I joined the fire service, stationed here with you, commendation, things were going well and then I fucked it up by one stupid evening cruising this seafront pretending to be a copper.

"My bad luck was reprimanding two guys for cycling on the pavement who turn out to be trainee solicitors. My good luck was you and dark Green making a possible conviction go away. The shame I felt was back. I internalised it, always have, then coming to work each Red Watch tour and there you were, my shame made manifest.

"The years our careers diverged were pretty good for me. I was never going to be Eddie Hart but I got promoted, got a nice place, was doing fine. I hoped our paths would never cross again, possible in this job, then the promotion to OIC at Langden. Couldn't turn it down even with you there. Then what, well best form of defence is attack, right?"

"Wow, you are one stupid cunt."

"Same again, gents?"

"Yea, same again and sorry for the language."

"No Eddie, if you say that then you have no idea of the power of shame. I've been having counselling."

Eddie spat beer on the pavement and laughed.

"That's it, fucking laugh at me."

"Clarence mate, so have I." He laughed again. "So have I. Drink your beer. Cheers."

"I can't drink all that. I'm still on my first."

"I'll drink 'em. I can walk home from here."

"Excuse me," said Clarence to the owner, the girl had left, "do you have gin?"

"Of course."

"Can I have a gin and tonic please?"

Eddie was still chuckling to himself when the G and T arrived. "What we do to one another, Clarence eh?"

"I know and I'm sorry, Eddie."

"No, no, it was a rhetorical question. I'm sorry too by the way."

"What for?"

"Well, I accused you of some bad shit."

Eddie started the fifth bottle.

"I meant generally how, you know, how we generally treat one another. Do you know Phillip Larkin?"

"I do, the best poet laureate we never had."

"Ah, I would never have put you down for a lover of poetry."

"I'm not, I remember you banging on about him when we worked together."

"I'm impressed."

"Man hands on misery to man/it deepens like a coastal shelf/get out as early as you can/and don't have any kids yourself."[8]

Eddie belched.

"Excuse me, so at least we are doing that right eh, no kids."

"Well, I'm not so sure."

"Why?"

"I've been seeing a woman, we have only met a few times, pictures or drinks but she really seems to like me. I can't get over it."

"Do you like her?"

"Oh, she is stunning, Eddie. I'm smitten and worried at the same time in case she has a change of heart."

"Go for it, Clarence and don't walk away, fight for her mate, fight for her."

"D'you want another?"

"Yea go one. I can walk from here too."

The owner cleared their table and set down fresh drinks. "She has a ten-year-old, Harvey."

"Father on the scene?"

"No, never has been."

"Excellent, instil in him the core values by which you lead your life while bringing him up, then when he's twenty-one he'll tell you he hates you and you've ruined his."

"Ever thought of writing an agony column?"

"We fuck our kids up with the best of intentions, we want them to be Catholic or agnostic musical or sporting a Tory or a commie a West Ham fan only a West Ham fan. We want success and happiness and intelligence, how that is longed for. With a keenness seldom realised in themselves parents push and push. The

---

[8] *This Be The Verse* by Phillip Larkin

kids then turn on the parental dream and everyone wonders what went wrong. The mums and dads that don't give a fuck are probably the best guiding lights."

"That is one cynical view, understandable but cynical. You do have to encourage a child though."

"Of course but temper it with realism. All this you can be whatever you want is bollocks. You ain't performing at La Scala if you can't fucking sing."

"So your parents fell into what camp."

"Both," said Eddie. "The one who cared with every fibre of her being and the one who simply couldn't."

"Cynical and self-pitying, can see why you're still single." He laughed again.

"Fuck off. I know. Being an only child don't help. You have a sister to ask if you're over reacting or not."

"My sister would rather grow a tail than talk to me. So what's the answer?"

"Friendship!" Exclaimed Eddie holding his drink aloft. "To friendship."

"I'm more worried about raising a child and then something happens to them like Sam."

Eddie nodded in agreement.

"I tried to speak to his parents but they refused to engage. I get they are upset but I'm also worried they are angry and might think about civil action against us," said Clarence.

"They won't."

"How do you know?"

"They know what I know and Lucy Holding knows." The owner put some nuts on the table. Clarence waited.

Eddie leant in. "Between you and me, right?"

"Right."

"Sam took the money."

"Bloody hell, Eddie. How on earth did you manage the outcome? I'm absolutely discombobulated."

"You're fuckin pissed. One beer and a couple of gins, lightweight."

"Seriously Eddie, tell me please."

"It was a strange brew. Confession, hubris, shame and luck."

"A heady cocktail."

"Do you want another one?" asked Eddie.

"Why not?"

"Let me order then I'll tell you."

With the drinks in he began.

"When Sam was hit, I got to him first. I'm sure he thought he was dying. He told me. I said, don't talk rubbish. He said, go and tell his parents. Then he slipped unconscious. Well, I was going to see his parents regardless of his confession. Wow, did I receive one frosty reception. You were in charge, you are responsible for my son now in an induced coma, you will have questions to answer. His mother was venomous.

"I had no option than to fight back so I told them what he said and the mood changed immediately. It was clear they knew nothing of the theft. It turns out our bright young star, our tip for the top, is a kleptomaniac. Has been all his life. Problems as a child, kicked out of Uni, stole his tutor's wallet, would you believe and now this. His father was conciliatory and asked if I could see a way to keep it quiet."

"How did you get the woman to drop the charges?"

"There was two things that bothered me about it all. Before Sam's accident. One thousand pounds to me seemed a credible amount for a professional working in the city so I kind of believed her but there was no mention in the local rag. Why didn't she sing from the rooftops? Might have panicked the Chief into an out of court settlement, no admission of guilt, all the usual shit. So I chanced my arm. Mr Brown was only too happy to give me two grand if I thought that would work. I just said yes and would worry later if it went Pete Tong. The luck was I found her at home."

"What did you say?"

"I told her the truth and of my suspicions. Turns out I was right. She's got a past."

"What?"

"Doesn't matter and I told her it wouldn't go any further if for another grand she concocted a story for the police and dropped the charges. To say I was on tenterhooks until you got the call that evening is an understatement. I phoned Nigel Brown. His sigh was audible down the line."

"You are a fucking genius, you should."

"If you say go for promotion, I'm off."

The two colleagues sat in silence, watching people pass by. A heavy bank of black cloud was forming over Kent. The high tide lapped gently against two deck chairs missed by the attendant. Eddie tried to recall his mother walking along this promenade, his memory melded into an amalgamation of childhood and later years.

He touched his wallet but decided not to get out her photo. It would place her at an exact moment in time. He didn't want that tonight, he felt he needed her for all time. He drained the last of his drink and looked at a drunk Clarence Siddall. "I'm serious, Clarence, no one, right?"

"No one, my lips ur zealed. Do you want another?"

"No and nor do you. Come on, it's a nice night. I'll walk you home."

Chapter 53

The following morning, Eddie needed Paracetamol. They never walked home but up to the train station where a couple of taxis were ranked up. When he got back to the flat, he sat on his balcony with a large Jameson. He went back over the evening with a slight feeling of unease.

Was Clarence genuine or had he got what he wanted to finish the Watch? He could usually judge character accurately, he thought, then look at Sam, got him wrong. It started to rain. A few spots soon became a downpour. Eddie went in and sat on the sofa to finish his whiskey. As he started to drift off, he was in the salon with Jane. She was looking at him in the mirror, he could feel her hand on his neck. Then it was black.

Eddie walked onto the station at the start of their second day. He noticed the ADO's door was open. The office was empty.

"Good night?" asked John Mullins, carrying his fire gear out to the bay.

"Slept on the sofa."

"Another argument with yourself."

"Yea," said Eddie.

Arthur Church came out of his room.

"Morning Eddie, listen do me a favour. They have transferred in a temporary replacement for Sam. She is in my room now. Same squad as Sam so not much experience but she volunteered to join us. Can you give her the introductory chat? I've got a phoned radio interview to announce my upcoming candidacy. Cheers."

Eddie changed quickly. He entered the station officers' room to see the Watch's latest addition reading a magazine.

"Morning."

"Morning, Sub."

She held up the mag. "Found it on the chair." Eddie smiled.

"I'm Eddie."

"Lindsey."

"The guvner tells me you volunteered to come over."

"Yea, I heard good things about this Watch."

"Really."

"Yea, good bunch, bit of a laugh and it's a busy station. To be honest, I was a bit bored where I was."

"You met anyone apart from me and Arthur so far?"

"Yea, Ken in the mess. He asked if I was a veggie."

"Are you?"

"No, my old man's a butcher. Give me meat and plenty of it."

"You knew Sam?"

"Yea, nice guy. He was the brainy one of the squad. We all thought he'd go far. Terrible. Shows you how easy it is to fuck up."

"Well, I'm sure you won't."

"Good, bloody hope not."

"So tell me about yourself. Why did you join?"

"Dunno really, bored driving for a living, seemed a good idea at the time. What you smiling at?"

"Dunno really," he said, mimicking her.

"Oh, I know everyone says how bad I talk."

"Come on," said Eddie. "I'll introduce you to the Red Watch."

The End

Printed in Great Britain
by Amazon

56033810R00112